TWISTED
THE GRIM TOWER DUET
PART ONE

Renee Rocco

reneerocco.com

TWISTED

Copyright © 2022 by Renee Rocco

All rights reserved

No part of this book may be reproduced in any form or by any electronic or mechanical means, including information storage and retrieval systems, without written permission from the author, except for the use of brief quotations in a book review.

This is a work of fiction. Names, characters, businesses, places, events, locales, and incidents are either the products of the author's imagination or used in a fictitious manner. Any resemblance to actual persons, living or dead, or actual events is purely coincidental.

Cover Design and Interior Design: Renée Rocco

Editor: Cassandra Higgins

Proofreader: Lisa Gillian

First Electronic Edition: August 2022

First Print Edition: August 2022

Printed in the United States of America

Warning

Welcome to my imagination, where the villains are the heroes. My stories may include triggers for some readers. Listing (the numerous) warnings here might be seen, to some, as spoilers.

For a list of warnings, please visit my website: https://reneerocco.com/content-warnings

For those of us who grew up secretly wishing the villains got the girl. We're the ones who want our fairytales filthy and our heroes tarnished.

"And for that one moment, everything was perfect … And then that moment ended."

— **Flynn Rider,** *Tangled*

Playlist

Glycerine by Bush
Mouth by Bush
The Undertaker by Puscifer
Darkside by Neoni
Unstoppable by Sia
Saddens by Enigma
Fumbling Towards Ecstasy by Sarah McLachlan
The Mummers' Dance by Loreena McKennitt
Demons by Imagine Dragons
Bring Me to Life by Evanescence
Tainted Love by Marilyn Manson
Bodies by Drowning Pool
Falling Away From Me by Korn

Listen to the full playlist
https://spoti.fi/3un4FB0

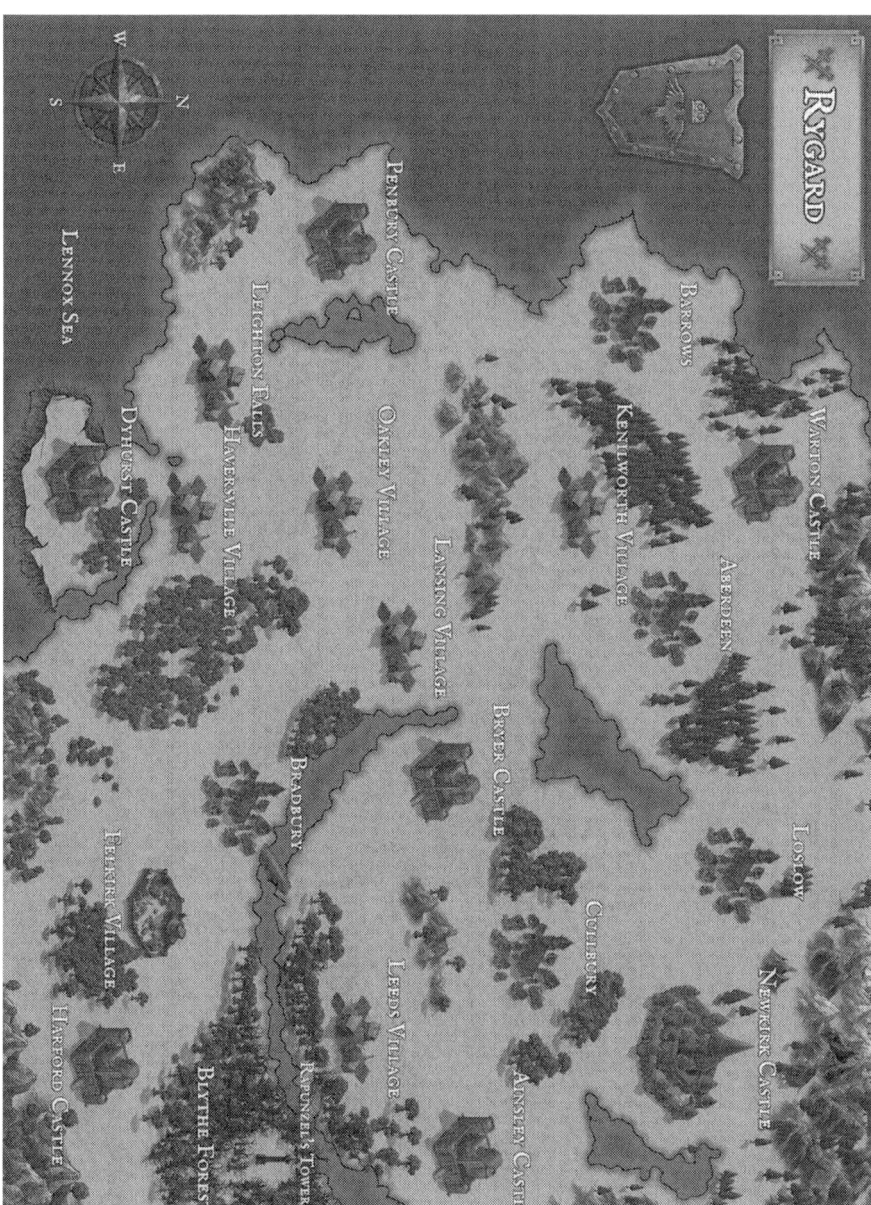

Chapter One

WREN

Twelve Years Old

Rumor has it Blithe Forest is cursed. They say an evil witch lives here, hidden somewhere among the ancient trees and twisted, thorny foliage. She's why most folks don't dare venture this far south from Leeds Village, much less cross the Merrie River. Scared, the lot of them. Not me. Papa says I'm fearless, though. Ma calls me reckless. But how can anyone be afraid on a day like this, when the sun is filtering through the canopy of trees, making the pollen sparkle like fine jewels? Besides, if she tries to do her foul magic on me, I'll… I'll…

I snatch a big stick lying on the river's bank and wield it like a soldier's sword. "That's right, witch," I threaten my imaginary foe. "I'll carve you to pieces."

Play-fighting with the air, I swipe, parry, and dodge, working up a sweat until I'm panting and my undershirt molds to me. I drag in giant lungfuls of muggy August air and toss my stick aside. I wobble on one foot as I peel off my battered black leather boot.

Much better.

I kick off the other boot before splashing in the cool water. The riverbed sucks at my feet, with the mud squishing between my toes. A rustle in the distance has me shoving a flop of brown hair off my brow. I shield my eyes against the glint of sun reflecting off the lazy river and spy a cloaked figure moving through the trees on the other side of the bank.

A cloak in this heat?

My adventurous spirit, which Ma swears will get me in trouble one day, draws me toward this suspicious enigma.

I glance at the sky, notice the sun's position, and realize it's late afternoon. Darn. I should start the trek back to Leeds. Ma will skin me alive for coming home filthy. Again. But curiosity has me tracking the shadowy figure. I compare my size to the person skulking through the trees. I have my father's build, tall and lean. At twelve, I stand a full head higher than most boys my age. Judging by me, it's easy to gauge that the person is too small to be a grown man but too large to be a child. This adds to the mystery—and the thrill of the chase.

I hop back on the bank and grab my boots as quietly as possible. I use the dense brush to conceal myself and dash along the river, following it to Peddler's Bridge. It's a rickety thing constructed of weathered wooden slats and frayed rope. It should have been torn down ages ago. No one uses it anymore since they built the new, sturdier Merchant's Bridge farther north. That one links Leeds Village to the big, busy town of Bradbury—it's also a safe distance from the witch's rumored evil sorcery.

Could it be *her* lurching in the woods?

The witch?

Darn again. I shouldn't have tossed away my stick. To be safe, I snatch another.

Keeping the lone figure in sight, I race along the bank. My bare feet step down hard on twigs, rocks, and dirt. Should pull on my boots, but I don't want to lose sight of the witch. Not that I put any stock in such a thing. I'm not a silly child who believes in fairytales. Still... It's curious how the people who venture this far south never return.

I grip my makeshift weapon tighter in my right hand, my boots dangling in the left. I slow my pace. Perhaps it's not such a good idea to follow the witch. But then I spot Peddler's Bridge, and I get a surge of courage. Or possibly it's my father's huntsman nature manifesting itself in me. Whatever the reason, I stay low and tiptoe my way across the bridge, leaping over the worst of the decayed planks. Hopefully, the river's rush disguises the groan of stressed lumber.

On the other side of the Merrie River, I dart behind a tree, watching as she—it's a *she* for sure—strides past me with a majestic glide to her steps. Wisps of long, chestnut hair billow from the hood of the black cloak that conceals her from head to foot. That hair reminds me of sinister fingers seeking the warmth of the sun.

She's quick, this one, as she heads toward the edge of Blithe Forest. *Blithe*. What an odd name for a place known for its grim reputation. I shake off the irony and keep my focus on the witch, and once she's beyond the cluster of towering trees, she simply...

...disappears.

My heart sinks to my feet like an anchor.

I struggle to swallow and drop to jam my dirty feet in my muddy boots. I can't wait to brag to my friends that I encountered the witch of Blithe Forest and survived. When I pop up, I spin left. Then right. I can't catch my bearings. My brows slam together in confusion. The bridge I crossed is now a tangle of dying, twisted trees. As if it vanished along with the witch.

What trickery is this?

The wily witch and her foul ways.

The son of Percy Kincaid shouldn't be frightened by the

terrifying tales racing through my mind of the lost souls wandering this forest.

With my heart beating like a hammer, I run. I pick a random direction, hope it's toward home, and run so fast my legs ache. Run until my lungs hurt from sucking in the heavy, damp air.

I run until I reach a glade where I see it...

It.

And skid to stop because it's so...

Lonely.

A stain against the bleak landscape. It sits by itself, rising from the ground to scrape the clouds. A circular tower that stands at least five stories, if not more. With its gray stones, black roof, and single silver spire that points like a needle straight to the sky, it's a dark streak that seems to have chased away every living thing, leaving nothing but this grim monstrosity standing in the center of the clearing.

"You can't be here."

I blink and spin, doubting I heard such an enchanting voice echo in this dead space. "Who said that?"

"I did." The musical notes of that voice flit above me.

Frowning, I shove the stubborn fall of hair from my eyes and glare at the tower, searching for the source. There's a single open window at the top, where a white curtain billows from the gentle summer breeze. I strain my neck to peer inside, but I'm met with darkness. I raise my stick like a sword, ready to defeat any threat.

"Show yourself, witch," I demand.

"I'm no witch."

I jab at the air. "Then why hide from me?"

"No one is supposed to know I'm here."

Lowering my arm, I tilt my head and scrunch my face in confusion. "You do realize by talking to me, you—"

"Yes, I know," she interrupts me again, this time with an almost sad-sounding sigh in her tone. There's a weird...scraping…sound coming from inside the tower. Like metal against stone, but it fades. Everything fades when I see her.

Her.

First, it's just the top of her head. Then she rises in the window like the dawn. More of her comes into view, the vision of her a punch right to my gut. The girl is…lovely. There's no other word to describe her, really. Especially not with the navy tunic contrasting her fair coloring and the plaited golden cord wrapped around her trim waist.

I wish I could see the color of her eyes, but she's far too high.

Her hair, though…

Her golden hair.

I've seen nothing so glorious in all my life.

"You're just a girl." Shocked, I let my makeshift weapon slip from my hand.

She must be my age if she's a day. She rests her elbows on the window's ledge and drops her chin on her upturned palms. There's something so…forlorn…about her. "And you're just a boy."

I bounce my gaze around the glade. At the tower, with no visible door, searching for answers to questions I haven't asked. Then back at her, and I'm struck again by the girl's fragile beauty. "What are you doing up there?"

She shrugs her shoulders. "I live here."

"You live here?"

She lifts her head from her hands and extends her arms to hoist herself higher, allowing me to get a better view of her. She comes way too far out of the window. Again, I hear that scraping, but my concern that she'll fall overrides my curiosity about the ominous sound. I step closer to the tower as if I can catch her if she tumbles.

"Aye, I do." Her hair—so long I can't tell where it ends—catches the sun's rays like spun gold. When she takes my measure, her expression, from what I discern from this distance, is pure curiosity. "May I ask you a question?"

"I give her a loose shrug. "Sure."

She peers at the ground and then back at me. "Tell me, what is the dirt like beneath your feet?"

"The dirt?" I repeat dumbly.

"Do you plan to repeat everything I say?"

Embarrassed, I find a rock to kick. "I suppose not."

"Good, because we don't have much time." Her smile is enchanting. "Please tell me, what does the dirt feel like?"

I find her question odd. Everyone knows what the darn dirt is like. "How can you not know?"

"I've never touched it."

Wait. What?

"Does your mama never let you outside to play?"

She leans out the window again. This time, she crosses her arms on the ledge and almost wistfully lays her chin on them. "I daresay I have never left this tower."

Shocked, I take a moment to comprehend her confession. I want to ask if she's a prisoner, but the question gets stuck in my throat. Instead, I crouch and snatch a handful of grass and dirt. I let it filter through my fingers in damp clumps. "After last night's rain, the air is hot and sticky. The dirt is still damp. It's warm and heavy in my hand." I break apart what's left and crumble the chunks. "When it's dry, it reminds me of dust. The grass is soft but firm, like…" I struggle to think of a way to describe it, but I don't know what she does or doesn't have in the tower. "Straw, I guess. Do you understand?"

"The same as what fills my bed?"

"Yes," I confirm.

"What's your name?"

The joy vanishes from her face. She steps back, the scrape of metal against stone faint with her movements. "I… I can't." She shakes her head. "You need to go now, before she returns."

"Okay, I'll leave." I hold up my dirty hands in surrender and walk backward, away from the tower. "I didn't mean to scare you."

"I'm not scared of you." She glances beyond me. At what lies behind me. "I'm scared *for* you."

My stomach coils in a knot. "Is this *she* the witch who cursed Blithe?"

A hesitant nod is her only answer.

I knew it.

I shouldn't have come this far south.

But if I hadn't, I'd have never found this tower.

I would not have met this lovely girl.

"I'm not afraid of witches." I pick up my stick and puff out my chest. "My name is Wren. Wren Kincaid. Our friendship is now a certainty, and as your friend, I promise you, I'll come back as often as possible. I won't leave you to stay here alone with the witch."

Her weak smile is an arrow shot straight into my heart. "Rapunzel." Her sweet voice drifts to me from the window. "My name is Rapunzel."

The novelty of the name rivals the mystery of the girl. "I'll see you soon, Rapunzel."

Chapter Two

WREN

Thirteen Years Old

"I hate when you sit like that."

"Like what, this?" Rapunzel, perched on the window's ledge, dangles one leg out of the tower. She swings it back and forth, with her bare foot scraping against the outer stone wall.

After a brutal winter, nature gifted Rygard with an early spring. Rapunzel has the pane thrown wide open, with the white curtain drawn aside. She is, as always, a vision, with her hair in a thick plait. And here I am, a grubby mess. But at least I scrubbed my face clean and dug out the dirt under my nails lest she think me a heathen. Nothing I can do to rectify the sad state of my clothes, though. My friends and I were sparring, and I took a tumble in the mud. She didn't mind that I came here filthy and even laughed when I told her how Peter, the blacksmith's son, got the better of me—again.

My stomach flip-flops at her precarious position. Darn her. I can't catch her if she falls. I may be strong, but she's too high. She'll splat on the ground. "Why must you scare me?"

"Because it's funny." The infernal girl keeps rocking her leg back and forth because apparently, she wants to age me before my time.

Good God, her leg is lovely.

Her pink tunic rode way up when she swung the limb out the window. I want to tell her to yank the material back in place, but the suggestion got lost on its way from my brain to my mouth. And although I'm afraid she'll tumble to her death, I can't help but admire her tiny bare foot before I drag my gaze along to her thigh.

Ogling her has my body reacting in a rather...uncomfortable...way. "Heck no, it's not funny. Especially not if I'm the one who has to scrape your brains off the grass."

I sound ridiculous, but I'm all sorts of flustered because of her damnable leg.

"Trust me, Wren, it's fine." Her laugh falls on me, and I curse the distance that separates us. "You sound like an old biddy."

"Oh yeah? Well… Well, you're acting like a brat," I counter, hoping my authoritative tone disguises my stumbling retort.

Rapunzel laughs louder, the sound delightful.

During one of my visits, she explained how the witch's curse on Blithe is strongest here, where she cast the spell that infects the forest. The ground is alive with Sybil's power, and when I grab a handful of dirt and mash it in my hands, I wish it were she I was crushing. After all, she's why Rapunzel is a prisoner. Not a day goes by when I'm not tempted to tell my parents about my mysterious friend, but whenever I try, I hear Rapunzel's voice in my head, begging me to keep silent.

"Would you be terribly sad if I fell?"

What an awful question. "Aye, Zee, I would." I push off the ground, where I've been sitting for the last hour. "Of course I would."

I would be devastated.

She swipes wisps of hair away from her face. "I'm sorry. Seems I'm full of melancholy questions this morning."

In the year I've known her, Rapunzel hasn't shown herself to be a cheerful person. Who would blame her for her melancholy? She's spent her life locked in this tower. Her feet have touched nothing but the stone of her floor. She's never felt the wind in her hair unless it's filtered through the single window where she views the world day after lonesome day.

And that world is restricted to the same landscape, changed only by the passing seasons, for the past thirteen years.

Besides Sybil, who took her from her family when Rapunzel was an infant, I'm the only other person she knows—and the witch is rarely here. I can't imagine how heavy the solitude must weigh on her.

The first—and only—time I asked about her family and why she was in the tower, Rapunzel panicked. She demanded I leave and never return. She even threatened to tell Sybil I visit her and warned me the witch would wipe this place from my mind. Erase Rapunzel from my memory. The very idea horrified me.

So, I promised.

I swore on my life and hoped I would die if I ever told a soul about her or this grim tower where she's forced to live.

Rapunzel is my cherished secret.

We're now in this together.

"What other melancholy questions have you asked?"

Finally, Rapunzel drags her leg inside and smooths her hands over the front of her tunic. I breathe easier with both of her feet on solid ground. She flips the braid over her shoulder. Shorter brown wisps, I've noticed, interlace with the much longer golden waves. As with everything else, I swallow the question of why the length and color difference lest I lose her.

"It's nothing, Wren, truly. Just silly ponderings I had no business asking."

"If it's nothing, share it with me," I dare to press.

She shrugs her slender shoulders and directs her face toward the sky. Framed in the large window with the sun hitting her just so, Rapunzel is a work of art. "I thought I discovered a way to rid myself of the reason I'm forced to stay hidden." She looks back at me, her sad smile heartbreaking. "Unfortunately, I was mistaken."

Suddenly, I'm ashamed of my freedom. "I'm sorry, Rapunzel."

"It's for the best."

"Best for everyone but you," I argue.

She doesn't disagree. "It's my burden to bear."

A burden much too heavy for her to carry alone. "What can I do to make you happy?"

Rapunzel thinks for a moment, tapping her finger against her chin. "Tell me more about your family, Wren, please."

I pick at one of the many calluses on my right palm—put there from long hours spent training with swords and bows. "You already know my mother is a midwife, and my father is a royal huntsman. What's left to tell?"

"Everything," she breathes. "I enjoy the stories you share with me of your grand adventures."

Adventures.

The inconsequential things I take for granted: daily school lessons, making mischief with my friends, grueling training sessions with weaponry, and household chores.

According to Rapunzel, these are my grand adventures.

I tell her the mundane details of my day. How I woke before dawn, ate a quick breakfast, and helped my mother with the chores while my father is away at Newkirk Castle visiting King John at court. I take what little of herself Rapunzel offers and allow her to live vicariously through me. In return, I spend time with this mysterious girl who has become my best friend.

"Nothing will compare to the adventures you and I will have once you are free of this place."

She rocks farther out. "Yes, Wren...such wonderful adventures await us."

Something in her tone sends a shiver down my spine. I don't know why.

Perhaps she doesn't believe she will leave this tower.

She's wrong.

The day she gains her freedom will be our first adventure together.

Chapter Three

WREN

Fourteen Years Old

"Once upon a time, there was an evil, old hag—"

"Wren, stop." Rapunzel, one hand planted on her hip, wags a scolding finger at me.

"Or what?" I ask on a laugh.

She *tsks* me, but I ignore her reprimand. The distance between us has increasingly become an itch I can't scratch. I'm training as a huntsman in earnest now, and it's taking up much of my time, making it difficult to sneak away from Leeds. The time between my visits and the space that separates us are living entities. Something tangible and ugly.

"Sybil is neither old nor evil."

I cock a brow at her assessment of her captor. "You have your opinion. I have mine."

"You've never seen Sybil. Therefore, you can't form a proper opinion," Rapunzel points out.

Sitting on the grass, I swipe my flop of brown hair out of my equally brown eyes and peer up at Rapunzel. As usual, she's perched on the edge of the windowsill. Today, she has a bright yellow blanket gathered around her lithe body. It's early spring, and the wind still carries a chill. I've finally grown large enough to inherit my father's old clothing. His deep green woolen jerkin works wonders to keep me warm during the endless hours spent outdoors.

"Not true," I counter. "I've seen the witch once. I'm convinced she led me to you."

"That's impossible." The note of skepticism in Rapunzel's voice drifts down to me on the breeze. "Sybil cloaks herself in magic. It renders her invisible to the eye." She thinks for a moment. "Not unless she wants to be seen."

I shrug, pulling up tufts of grass. "Maybe Sybil wanted me to find you." Rapunzel's measured silence draws my gaze from the ground to her. She's staring back at me, her expression peculiar. "What's wrong?"

"Nothing." Rapunzel slips off the window's ledge and retreats into the tower. "I'm tired, Wren. You'll come back soon, won't you?"

"Always, Rapunzel."

Before the promise finishes leaving my mouth, she's already gone from the window.

Chapter Four

WREN

Sixteen Years Old

Four years.

I've been coming to the tower for four years.

In the beginning, it was easy to sneak away from Leeds before the intrusion of responsibilities. Now? With my schooling complete, I hunt with my father. He pushes me harder, with each trip into the surrounding areas strengthening me. They make me sharper. Better. During our last outing, I felled a full-grown stag with a single arrow to the heart. My father was never prouder. It wasn't my first kill, but it was indeed my most impressive.

No, my first kill inadvertently led me to Rapunzel. How I bragged to my friends that I was a great hunter because I caught a coyote. My boast prompted them to dare me to venture into Blithe Forest. Unable to back down from the challenge, I walked farther than ever I had.

Until I reached the Merrie River, where I spied the witch on the opposite side of the bank.

And then I found myself in the glade—and the rest, as the

storytellers say, is history.

By the time I made it back to Leeds, my mother was worried sick since I'd been gone so long. My father arrived home soon after. He punished me right good for scaring her. Made me do double my chores for the entire week, but it was worth it because I met Rapunzel.

Rapunzel, with her golden hair, pale skin, and sad smile.

Rapunzel, with her secrets.

But I have a secret as well.

Percy Kincaid believes I'll replace him as King John's favorite. That I'll follow in his footsteps and become a royal huntsman. My father is wrong. Although I intend to become a master archer, I'll use my skills to get Rapunzel out of this tower and take us far away from here.

Far enough that Sybil's magic can never reach us.

"You're quiet today, Wren." Rapunzel sits straddling the ledge, her right leg dangling out the window.

My nerves can't take it and I have to turn away. If anything were to happen to her…

There would be no me without Rapunzel.

But it's impossible to keep my gaze off her for long. It drifts back on its own accord, and as always, I notice how she's grown over the years. Her body has developed, her delicate curves filling out her green tunic. And damn it if her skirt hadn't ridden up her thigh. My body, also matured, reacts to the sight of her shapely leg and bare foot swinging back and forth. She's sat this way many times before, but it's only these last couple of months that it's become unbearable to see this much of her flesh.

I stiffen and shift on the ground, resisting the need to adjust my cock to a more comfortable position within the crotch of my brown breeches. "I could say the same of you."

She heaves out a sigh loud enough to reach me. "I'm simply enjoying the day."

"How long do we have?"

Rapunzel stares beyond me, out toward the forest behind me. "Sybil won't return for hours."

With my legs crooked, I rest my arms across my knees and pray Rapunzel can't see her effect on me. "Where'd she go this time?"

"Not sure."

She's lying.

After all this time, I know Rapunzel's tells.

Even now, she still protects her secrets.

Once I free her from the tower, I'll shatter every remaining barrier between us. Finally earn her trust. Until then, I'll leave her to whatever mysteries she believes she needs to keep.

"Did you forget what today is?" I ask with a *tsk*.

Even from a distance, I see her frown. "Today?"

I stand and wag a finger at her. "Rapunzel, you forgot."

She pulls in her leg, and I want to groan at the loss of that smooth flesh. There's the familiar faint scrape of metal against stone. "Will you leave me in suspense indefinitely?"

I reach into the pocket of my breeches and extend my arm. She watches, transfixed, as I open my hand, palm up. "These remind me of you."

Rapunzel grips the ledge of the window, leaning out dangerously far. "Hold it higher, Wren, please."

There's a note of panic in her tone as if she'll lose this moment forever.

I stand on my tiptoes as if that alone can bring it closer. "It's a peony. They grow in my mother's garden." I stuff the battered pink flower back in my pocket. "I'll give it to you on the day you leave this tower."

Her smile drops. "I'd like that." She licks her lips, and by the way she's gripping the ledge, I can tell she's holding on too tight. "But you still have yet to tell me why today is special."

I place a hand over my heart. "Happy sixteenth birthday, Rapunzel."

Chapter Five

WREN

Eighteen Years Old

"You see me. I see you. Your turn to tell me true." Rapunzel's husky voice falls like rain from the tower. It's a simple rhyme. A silly game children play in Leeds. It's one I hope will help loosen Rapunzel's tongue.

"Let me think…" I tap my index finger against my chin as I pace the glade. The unseasonably warm October afternoon is a welcome relief after yesterday's chill. I stripped away my thick, brown woolen jerkin. It's resting next to the longbow King John gifted me when my father presented me at court on my eighteenth birthday. This brings to mind the perfect confession… "My father believes I'm ready to take my place in John's army. But, of course, I won't go."

"That's foolish, Wren." Rapunzel, perched on the windowsill, hugs her yellow blanket tight around herself. "Do you plan to stay in Leeds the whole of your life?"

I shrug. "Maybe."

"You need to go."

Twisted

My face drops into a scowl. "If I go, I'll be gone for months. Perhaps even years."

The king is notorious for keeping his garrison close. If John and my father hadn't been friends since they were children, Percy Kincaid never would have been granted permission to move himself and his wife out of Newkirk Castle. Even now, the king complains how my father 'abandoned' him when he left court to move to Leeds.

Rapunzel turns her face to the sky. "I'm aware of that fact, Wren."

Of course she is because we've discussed this, the possibility of me going off to the king's court in Kent. It's what I thought I wanted since I was old enough to lift a bow. Until I met Rapunzel, and I decided I wanted something else. Now, the prospect of joining John's royal household is...unacceptable.

"And you're fine with me living a two-day ride from here?" I spit out the question, angry at how she could flippantly cast me aside. "Because that's how long the king will expect me to stay at court."

"I have to be." Rapunzel twirls a length of her hair, her gaze everywhere but on me. "It's unfair for me to expect you to plan your life around me." She drops her hair and finally meets my glare. "I've told you repeatedly, Wren, I cannot leave this tower, *ever*."

Frustrated, I scrub a hand over my face. Spite gets the better of me, and I sneer, "Bronwyn Fraser asked me to kiss her."

Rapunzel stiffens in the window. Then she squares her shoulders and notches her chin. "And did you?"

Her voice is as brittle as an old leaf, crumbled to dust and scattered on the wind.

"Yes," I confess.

Because in a moment of weakness, I gave in to curiosity and experienced my first kiss.

The yellow blanket falls away, and even from this distance, I can tell Rapunzel is shaking. "I see."

Never in my whole life have I wished for the power to take back my words, even as anger rips through me.

"Do you? Do you really? You don't want me to suffer from guilt for living, but when my lips touched hers, I hated myself." I doubt she understands what her stubbornness is doing to me. How her insistence on remaining Sybil's captive is killing me. "I keep coming here, in the cold, and the rain, and the snow. To visit you. Because I... Because we're friends. And now you tell me I need to go to court? To go off and live a life I don't want? What happens when a pretty girl asks for more than a kiss? What then, Rapunzel?"

If I climbed the tower and slapped her across the face, I don't think it would hurt her more than my rant.

"You need to go, Wren."

"Come away with me, Rapunzel," I rush out—and once the plea leaves my mouth, it's as if a burden lifts from me.

Rapunzel steps back from the window. "I can't."

Those two words fall on me like arrows. One slams into my heart. The other pierces my soul.

"You mean you won't." I storm over to where I left my belongings and snatch up my jerkin, longbow, quiver and arrows. "*You* should have been my first kiss, but you're too damn scared to leave this tower."

When I turn to walk away, she calls my name. I stop dead and spin to face her. She looks so fragile and lonely, framed in the window.

"Say it," she demands, her voice shaking.

Oh, God, she's crying.

I made my Rapunzel cry.

"The rhyme," she shouts. "Say it!"

Right at this moment, I'd carve out my heart and hand it to her if it would dry her tears.

"You see me. I see you. Your turn to tell me true."

Rapunzel reaches for something near her feet. That familiar scraping, the one I heard a hundred times over the years, finally —*finally*—has a source. Draped in her tiny hands is a length of thick chain. She sets her bare foot on the ledge, revealing a metal cuff clamped around her left ankle.

Sybil, that monster, tethered Rapunzel to the tower.

She drops the chain, and it makes a terrible rattle and thud when the links crash against stone. "You have no idea how dangerous I am."

"You're right, Rapunzel, I don't!" I roar. "I don't, because for six fucking years, I've shared all of myself with you. During that time, I've learned nothing about you other than your favorite color, food, and other frivolous bullshit. I know nothing of substance about you. You talk of us being friends. I've done the work for both of us."

Again, I turn to leave, and this time when I walk away, I don't stop.

No matter how desperate her screams are for me to come back.

The trek to Leeds has never been so arduous and lonely.

Chapter Six

WREN

Twenty Years Old

"This must be a proud day for you, Percy." King John winks at my father while he tugs on the neck of my new, crisp brown jerkin. The soft leather slides through his calloused hands. The ruby adorning his finger—as large as a baby's fist—gleams under the glow of the candlelight. "And for you, Wren."

"Yes, your majesty. Of course." My reply is by rote, my mind elsewhere.

I'd rather be freezing my balls off in a cursed forest while gazing at an enchanting blonde. Instead, my worst nightmare has come to pass. The day has arrived when John is bestowing upon me an 'honor' I neither want nor intend to keep.

"Bah." Rygard's gregarious king dismisses my proper etiquette with a wide grin. "None of that formality between us. Percy and I are old friends." He steps back and examines me, his keen blue eyes missing nothing. They're a sharp contrast to his black hair and sun-tanned skin. An active king who spends as much time ruling from his throne as he does on the back of his horse. "That makes us friends as well." He may be tall, but he lacks my stature. His lips thin to a somber line, and his expression speaks of a story I can't decipher. "This kingdom has its secrets, Wren. Secrets some men might be desperate enough to kill to protect."

An odd remark.

And the way his eyes slice into me... I swear the man sees past my skin and bones. As if he pierces my soul and extracts my deepest secret.

My Rapunzel.

I pull my brows into a deep frown. "I'm sure I don't know what you mean, Your Majesty."

John leans low, his lips uncomfortably close to my ear. "Your parents have always enjoyed the privilege of my esteem. You would be wise to maintain my affection as well." He retreats, and the tense moment, if indeed that's what it was, goes as quickly as it came.

He steps up on a dais, his jewels gleaming like stars against the rich hue of his clothing. Only the best for the king, with his deep blue surcoat, with its gold trim. This is a leader who commands the respect of his soldiers through solid leadership and brilliant military strategy. He's a monarch beloved by his people for restoring the kingdom after his father's tumultuous reign.

Old King Henry was destroying Rygard one terrible decision at a time. He drained the country's coffers on frivolity and led our people into a fool's war that cost the kingdom many a father and son. Anyone who opposed his mad rule or he suspected of treason was executed without trial, with their entire family slaughtered along with them.

Some claim John orchestrated Henry's demise.

Those same people say my father carried out John's will.

An arrow felled Henry, struck with precision through the mad king's right eye. It knocked him clean off his horse amid the chaos of one of his needless battles. Only one man, they claim, could make that shot.

Percy Kincaid.

John's closest friend, who later retired from his position to settle in the countryside, removed from the decadence and intrigue of court life.

"I'm always your humble servant, my lord." This too, I say by rote, still rattled by the king's whispered remark.

No—it was a warning. Or perhaps I'm reading too much into it?

The gold crown nestled in his brown curls stays firmly in place when John shakes his head. "My boy, you don't possess a humble bone in that big body of yours."

"Aye, John, you got that right," my father confirms with a laugh.

John puffs out his chest and gives my father a smirk. "I'm always right, Percy." He waves his hand through the air, motioning to the cavernous room where his gilded throne sits. "That's why God appointed me king."

"God also made you an arrogant ass," my father quips.

No one else would dare speak to our liege so disrespectfully. Even I suck in a sharp breath and hold it, waiting for King John's reaction.

Damn it all if the king doesn't flip my father the middle finger. Discreetly, of course. "I should cut out your tongue."

"Mary would have your head if you sent me home to her missing certain body parts."

Issuing a direct threat to the king is an instant death sentence—except if it comes from Percy Kincaid.

John slaps his hand over his heart. "Not my sweet Mary. Besides, I think her not having to hear your grating voice and participate in your dull conversation is a better trade-off than anything else you could do with that talentless tongue."

My father's laughter fills our immediate space, set apart from

Twisted

the courtiers gathered for today's ceremony. "Your sweet Mary has a vicious temper, to be sure. Now get on with it. I'd like to return home to her and show her how well I can have a conversation."

It's a struggle not to smile at their easy banter. But the king's forlorn gaze bounces between my father and me, ending their merriment. "Wren, seeing you and Percy makes me wish I had spent my younger years differently. I fear for Rygard when I'm gone."

"There is still time to produce an heir, Your Majesty."

He slides his gaze to Queen Eleanor, who stands with her ladies-in-waiting at the far end of the hall. The fear radiating from her is palpable. The stunning young woman, with her long black hair and striking blue eyes, quickly looks away. It's no secret theirs is a loveless marriage. Nineteen—seventeen when she wed the king—she denies him access to her chamber. Rumor has it John's…affections…are too much for our timid queen.

John adored Queen Anne and still mourns her and the stillborn child she died birthing. No wonder he hasn't fully embraced his second wife, regardless of her youth and beauty. How could he when his heart lies with his lost family?

"We shall see, won't we, Wren?" Then he beckons a page. The boy rushes over and stands proud before the king, holding a plain black box for John to take. "Now, let us begin." John turns to his courtiers. "We gather today to welcome and honor Wren, son of Percy Kincaid."

The room falls silent while the king speaks. All gazes are on our hale and hearty liege. On my father and me, standing below him, dressed in our finest clothing, sewn by the loving hand of Mary Kincaid.

"From this day forward, you are a royal huntsman." John's voice echoes throughout the chamber when he addresses me. The king raises a silver arrowhead for all to see. Then he pins it to my jerkin. Gives me a playful wink before becoming serious once again. "Turn and be recognized, Wren Kincaid of Leeds."

At his command, the crowd of two dozen courtiers applauds me. The sound is vulgar when, even now, my thoughts drift to Blithe. I'd rather listen to the husky echo of Rapunzel's voice resonate in the sterile glade. Stare up at her flawless face instead of the garish visages of John's courtiers. With their fine clothing, irrelevant conversations, and false laughter—all of it is…nothing.

Rapunzel is everything.

This ceremony… This honor. This meaningless position John appointed me… I'll use it to become a better…me. To become stronger. Quicker. More stealthy.

Lethal.

To prepare me for when it becomes my responsibility to protect Rapunzel. Because despite her protests, the day will come when I visit her, and I won't leave that glade alone.

Chapter Seven

WREN

Twenty-One Years Old

"Rapunzel!" My roar echoes across the glade. It reverberates off the gray stone of the tower. Weaves between the freezing rain pelting Blithe. I wait a long while before I snatch a rock and whip it at the windowpane. Of course, it lands short, falling to the saturated ground. "To hell with you, then," I snarl.

I turn to leave, fury and frustration and…anguish…ripping through me like a violent tide.

"Wren."

I skid to a halt.

Squeeze my eyes shut.

My heart batters my sternum.

I haven't heard her voice in months. *Months*. After our last argument, I came thrice. Thrice she stubbornly refused to come to the window. And pride kept me from begging for just one moment of her time—until my father lay dying. I screamed up to her empty window that he was sick. Came here once a day for six days needing just a glimpse of her to help me through the worst moments of my life, but she denied me.

But now she's at the window, and her voice—the loveliest sound in all the wretched world—resonates around me.

The rain stings my face as I turn. My God, she's so damn lovely. A drop of beauty on this ugly day. "Now you show yourself? *Now*, after all these days?"

She bows her head, that glorious golden hair tumbling forward. Then she looks at me and gathers her yellow blanket around herself like a shield. It's the same blanket she's had for years. I swear, I think I see a tear slip down her cheek. Or it could be the rain. Right now, I neither know nor care.

"I'm sorry," she rasps.

"Fuck your *sorry*." I step backward, shaking my head. "Poor, lonely Rapunzel, locked in her tower, too much of a coward to help herself. Poor Rapunzel, too afraid of her terrible secret to share it with her best friend." I spit at the tower as I inch farther away, toward the mouth of the glade. "You never trusted me. I gave you everything. But you couldn't even give me a moment of your time when I needed you. And why? Because we fight? It's what we do now, Rapunzel. Because you won't leave, and I can't watch you throw your life away."

Rapunzel's hands uncurl from the blanket. It drops away, and when she grabs the ledge, her fingers bite into the frame as if to steady herself against the battery of my words. "It's not like that, Wren."

"He's dead!" My bitter shout slices through the wind and rain sharper than a blade. "My father is dead, and there's nothing left for me here. I would have stayed. For you, Rapunzel. I would have done anything for you. Torn down this tower, stone by stone, for you. But you don't want freedom, and you don't want me. I hope you rot in there, you selfish bitch."

My boots sink in the mud, with the sodden ground wrapping around the black leather like fingers to keep me from walking away. I have to fight for each step. My longbow and quiver are a comforting weight against my back as I go, with Rapunzel's desperate calls echoing behind me as I leave.

"Wren, wait!" she cries. "Please don't go. Not like this. *Please*. Please come back. I'm sorry. *Wren!*"

Her plea bounces off my fractured heart. Not once as my father lay dying was she there to comfort me through the loss. Not once did I have her to console me while I watched his body rot from within. Each time I came to Blithe over the last six days, I risked missing my father's last breath for the consolation found only with her.

Her rejection struck deep.

So deep, it severed something that can't be stitched back together.

I was Rapunzel's sole breath of freedom. I'll take that with me when I go, and I hope my memory suffocates her.

Chapter Eight

WREN

Twenty-Four Years Old

Every man has a limit to his patience.

I surpassed mine years ago.

Even Dax and Quinn give me a wide berth now, and we've grown as close as brothers. They don't fuck with me on days when my nerves are raw. Like tonight, when I'm more on edge than usual. Or when I'm drunk, a state I'm rarely in because I don't enjoy giving up control. But the bottle is always my favorite companion on *this* day. Ale drowns the memories of *her*. It washes away the sting of the lost years spent believing *she* cared for me as much as I adored *her*.

Goddamn, this day.

Her twenty-fourth birthday.

I lift the bottle to my lips, but before I take another generous swallow, I say a silent, mock toast to *her*.

May your fucking hair dip into your chamber pot while using it.

The annoying buzz of the tavern surrounds me as I swig the ale and drift my gaze over the motley crew crowded inside The

Cup and Cross. Prostitutes. Outlaws. Murderers. Mercenaries. Drinking shoulder to shoulder. Because God help anyone who causes trouble while inside Adele Stafford's establishment.

She'd have no problem even taking Quinn to task, and my friend surrendered his soul to a demon—literally.

I found Quinn naked and bloody, curled in a fetal position on the side of a road. Only months out of Leeds, I had no idea what to make of him. His body radiated with a malevolent force he couldn't control. It was killing him from the inside out, and if I hadn't stumbled upon him when I did, it would have consumed him. I stayed by his side and helped him through those first torturous months while he fought to master the power he sacrificed everything to obtain.

For that, Quinn gave me his unequivocal loyalty.

Dax joined us soon after. Him, we came upon running for his life, bare-assed, from an angry old lord. Said lord caught Dax fucking his wife in their marital bed. Although we're not known for picking up naked strays, we made an exception for this one. Any man who can laugh with his cock flapping in the wind while being chased by a furious husband wielding a sword would, no doubt, fit in well with our two-person band of misfits.

We weren't wrong.

Dax and Quinn have two things in common. Both are former knights in the royal army.

They deserted rather than destroy Rygard.

Also, they despise John with the same fervor as I do.

Once more, I lift the bottle of ale to my lips, welcoming the promise of *blackout* drunk that slides down my throat. Across the worn, uneven planks of the table, Dax is talking to me, but I'm not listening. He always talks. I'm waiting for the day his jaw comes unhinged and falls clean off. Right now, though, I would sew his mouth shut if it granted me a moment's peace from his incessant conversation.

My God, for a renegade, Dax is too cheerful by half.

Half draped over the battered table, he's yelling over the din of voices. He stabbed the tip of his dagger into the soft wood so the weapon sticks straight up. His cup is empty—a major transgression. Quinn, lounging beside him on the bench, beckons over a server. The pretty girl's blonde hair fuels my temper as she sashays toward our table.

"More ale, girl," Quinn demands.

She's not intimidated by Quinn's gruff demeanor, and when she leans low, her ample chest damn near spills from atop her tight blue bodice. "Of course, milord."

Quinn snatches her by the wrist, his fingers with their black, vine-like markings, like he dipped them in ink—the aftermath of his deal with the demon—bite into her pale flesh. He yanks her closer, jostling her jug of ale. The brown liquid sloshes over the rim, splashing to the stone floor. The scar that cuts down his right cheek undulates when he clenches his jaw. "I'm no one's fucking lord."

Dax comes forward, ready to pry the poor woman away from him if need be. I, however, watch with a smirk, confident Quinn won't do more than scare her half to death. In my opinion, she deserves it for having the audacity to look like *her*.

Rapunzel.

Fuck.

I swore I wouldn't say her name, not even in the privacy of my mind.

Desperate to switch the subject lest my temper rise to a dangerous degree, I marvel—for the hundredth time—at more pleasant thoughts. Like how my life changed since leaving Leeds. I walked away with only the clothes on my back and a handful of shillings. Now, I have brothers and a sanctuary in southern Rygard, far removed from John's prying eyes. Our collective reputation of being a thorn in the king's side has spread, and everywhere we go, those who know us revere us.

Or fear us.

I also learned something from Quinn. It's a rumor, really. One that came to him from Queen Eleanor herself.

My father didn't die from a sudden illness.

John poisoned him—I've spent the last three years trying to discover why he assassinated his dearest friend.

It's also when my fight against the bastard began.

"More ale," the girl repeats with a nod at Quinn. Her blue eyes are wide, and a complacent grin lifts her plump lips. "Of course," she stammers. "I won't make the mistake again."

"No, you will not." Quinn releases her arm with a shove.

Dax catches the woman and steadies her. She fills their cups, her hands trembling. Quinn's roughness left a red mark around her wrist. "Will there be anything else?"

Leave it to Dax to smooth over a tense situation. He slides a hand down her back, tracing his fingers over her blue bodice. "Don't you worry about Quinn, sweetling. He's full of hellfire, but if you stay out of his path of fury, you'll be fine."

She arches her back against his touch but turns a blistering shade of red. "Dax Stafford, if you don't remove your hand from my person, I'll march upstairs and tell your mother you're manhandling me."

Dax takes his time complying, stroking his way to the small of her back before retreating. "Snitch."

She slaps his hand. "Lecher."

"Damn right," he drawls with a wink. He tugs at her cream-colored skirt to pull her back when she attempts to walk away. He wraps an arm around her waist and hugs her against his massive body, forcing her to hold her jug high. When she gifts him with a smile, he answers with his typical depravity. "Meet me upstairs later. I'll show you real manhandling."

Talia untangles his arm from around her waist, having already lost the battle against Dax's charm. "Promise you won't tell your mother."

All the man need do is crook a finger, and women run to him.

It's his pretty face and striking gray eyes. The disheveled mop of brown hair doesn't hurt. Women can't resist him. Also, his merry disposition makes him seem deceptively harmless when I've witnessed him kill men with less care than when a person crushes an insect.

Dax slaps a hand over his heart. "It shall remain our secret, dear Talia." He shoots a devious look at Quinn and me. "Unless you'd like it to remain between the three of us."

"Cheeky bugger," she scolds him, then turns to me. "Another bottle for you, Wren?"

"I'm good." Actually, I'm far from good. I'm piss-drunk and angry because I hate this fucking day.

As Talia strides away, I blink against the faint glow of the wall sconces. The light cuts the smokey interior, and when the wooden door flies open and a mountain of a man storms in, he slams it shut behind him. He joins a small group of tradesmen at a nearby table. But above all, the aroma of roasting pig overpowers the stink of sweat from the unwashed bodies gathered here.

Mine included.

Dax, Quinn, and I are, ourselves, fresh off the road. We delivered Hubert Yardley to the constable and collected the middling bounty. What happens to the horse thief now is up to the law. Given how Lansing handled such a crime in the past...

Yardley will get a light slap on the wrist, at best. But at least we got paid, and the horse he stole was returned. Win for everyone.

The Cup and Cross thrives because of Lansing's relaxed take on lawlessness. It's one of many villages whose exuberant taxes buy the king's indifference. It's the perfect marriage of John's greed and the people's desire for freedom. Unfortunately, it also makes Lansing a beacon for the less scrupulous, which makes its streets unsafe.

I finish the last of my ale in a single swallow and settle into a comfortable numb. My limbs are heavy, my mind slow, and when I catch pieces of a conversation, it's a chore to make sense of what I hear.

"A girl," someone says. "...captive by a witch."

"What did you say?" I demand of Dax, thinking it's my friend who spoke.

The blonde warrior points at himself. "Me? I was telling Quinn how I think my left testicle is larger than my right." He stands and begins to unlace his breeches. "Here, I'll show you."

"Pull out your cock, and this time I'll chop the fucking thing off." I swivel on the bench, the action sending the room into a spin. I need to slap my palm on the table to steady myself when I stand. "Who the fuck mentioned a witch?"

The tavern goes silent. Serving wenches skid to a stop. Every eye focuses on me, but I'm too deep in the bottle to give a damn.

"Sit your drunk self down, Wren." Quinn points to the bench, growling. "Before you end up on your ass."

"I'm steady enough." To prove I'm sure of foot, I pull the dagger from its sheath at my left hip and do a slow turn. "If I have to ask again, I start cutting throats until I get an answer."

"What's this?" Adele comes pounding down the stairs, her ample bosom almost smacking her in the face with each footfall. With its gold trim, the blood-red tunic must be held by God's hand to keep those breasts from spilling out. And then I realize I'm ogling Dax's mother's bosom and swiftly look away. "Wren, why are you wielding a weapon in my tavern?"

Even drunk, I wince at the reproach in her tone. "Trying to get an answer to a question."

She reaches the bottom of the stairs. "Is that so?"

"Yes, Adele, that's so."

She huffs out a grunt. "What was the question?"

Before I repeat it, Dax leaps in. "Seemed someone said something about a witch, and now Wren is in a snit."

Her eyebrows shoot to her graying hairline. "A witch?"

"Aye," I growl out. I point my dagger at the crowd. "I need to know who said it."

Adele shrugs. "You heard the man." She walks toward me. Covers my hand with hers and gently forces me to lower the dagger. "Not a drop of ale flows until—"

"It was me." A man tentatively rises at the table beside ours. Everything about him is plain and drab, someone I would have overlooked if he stood directly in front of me. "I said it."

"Well, now." Adele claps her hands. "That's settled." Her gaze cuts me. "Consider this your warning about brandishing a weapon in The Cup and Crown. I'll not tolerate it twice, especially not from a friend of Dax's."

Not only am I duly chastised, but I believe she'll gut me if I dare disobey her rule again.

Sliding the dagger into its sheath, I give her a curt nod. "Apologies, Adele."

"Accepted. Once," Adele warns.

I realize how close I came to ruining my relationship with a woman who has treated me like a son since the day I walked into her tavern with her son two years ago. That day, I brought nothing with me but the clothes I was wearing and a bad attitude resting heavy on my shoulders.

She strides away, and the tense moment ebbs. Conversations recommence.

I grab the slender man by the front of his shit-brown tunic, careful not to bring forth Adele's wrath twice. "What do you know about captives and witches?"

His face is ashen, his blue eyes wide. When he shakes his head, his greasy red hair scrapes his shoulders. "Only rumors."

I tilt my head and lift a brow. "If you want to keep your tongue, you'll repeat those rumors to me."

"Yes, yes. Of course," he stammers. "I passed through Oakley and Kenilworth, and even farther north, and chatter there is that King John searches for a witch."

His words curdle my insides like spoiled milk.

"What would the king want with a witch?"

He swallows loudly, his throat bobbing. "They say she holds a woman captive."

My rotten insides now feel like they're slithering up my throat, clawing for an escape. "And why does King John want this woman?" I keep my voice low enough that my words stay between us.

The man blinks at me, eyes now full of fear. He drags in a shaking breath before whispering, "The rumors didn't say." Then he mumbles so low that I must strain to catch his confession. "But between us, I heard tell this woman has the power to heal the sick, even the dying. That she keeps the witch young."

My fingers open as if on their own accord. My arms fall to my sides, and I stumble backward a few steps. The man scurries away, but I give him no notice. The tavern fades. I shuffle to the table and drop on the bench, dislodging the hurt I've kept caged for three miserable years.

A woman who can heal the sick—the dying.

While my father suffered, Rapunzel possessed the ability to cure him. But she hid in her tower and kept this gift to herself.

I never hated Rapunzel. Yes, her rejection hurt. But hate her? Never. Not until this very moment. Fuck her, and fuck King John because I know something he doesn't. I know where that selfish bitch is.

Rapunzel owes me a debt.

She owes me my father's life.

Chapter Nine

WREN

It takes a day and a half of hard riding to reach Leeds from Lansing.

The first thing I see is smoke, and my stomach coils. Each breath is suddenly laborious. The stench of burnt wood and straw is an assault as Dax, Quinn, and I drive our horses through the charred remnants of the village. We're met with the sickening sight of the once-bustling town reduced to rubble. The village green and market are destroyed, with the bodies of people I've known all my life littering the streets, their carcasses mutilated beyond recognition.

A handful of soldiers linger, draped in John's colors, their tabards sprayed with the blood of the innocents they slaughtered. I pull free my sword, and without thought or hesitation, I attack. I gallop Frenzy toward the men, hearing Dax and Quinn follow close behind me. Together, we cut them down as easy as batting away flies. But our attack draws out three additional soldiers from one of the last remaining intact buildings. Quinn shouts something, but I can't hear him past the rush of blood roaring in my ears.

Because I know what I'll find here.

I know.

"Wren, look at me, damn you!" Quinn's demand whips me out of my stupor. I blink hard and turn to my left, where he's seated atop his black destrier.

"Finish them," I sneer, even as the need to kill them myself burns hot.

"She's alive," Quinn assures me, but the words don't match the edge in his black eyes.

An ocean of doubt flows through my body as I break away from my friends. Kicking Frenzy into a run, I weave the horse through bloodstained, trampled streets. Around ransacked and ruined homes. Survivors call to me, their strangled voices faint echoes as they lie bleeding on the dirt. They reach out to me, pleading for help. Forced to ignore them, I'm desperate to find my mother. My gut coils tighter the closer I get to home. Sweat trickles a steady path down my face, and when I swipe hair away from my brow, my gauntleted hand comes away wet.

Perspiration?

Tears.

No matter. I don't care.

Houses this far north, away from the center of the village, were spared. A spark of hope flares inside me, and I send a silent plea to God.

Let her be alive if You have a shred of mercy in Your heart.

I slow my pace when I round the armory. The modest home where I spent two decades of my life comes into view. The coil loosens, and I exhale a relieved breath at the sight of the pristine exterior.

The door lies open and a curse whispers from my lips.

Jumping off my steed, I race toward the entrance but skid to a stop before entering. So many memories rip through my mind as I inch my way forward. I lick dry lips and swallow hard. Once. Twice. Then heave when I see a smear of blood among the muddy footprints on the stone floor.

Mercy.

There is no such thing in this realm.

There are only the lies fed to us on the silver tongue of a cruel king.

The coppery tang of blood thickens the air as I trudge through the main room. A cooking fire still smolders in the hearth. It's sickening how perfectly preserved everything is, as if my mother stepped out for a moment while preparing her evening meal...

...except for the drops of blood on the table and the overturned pot with stew puddled on the floor.

Numb legs carry me toward my mother's bedroom, following a pair of large, bloody boot prints. The sudden rush of adrenaline makes me sway like a drunkard, but I regain my balance. I charge forward as rage and desperation clash when I reach the threshold and see her lying prone on the floor.

Mary Kincaid. The foundation of our family.

The woman who was a light to everyone who knew her. A pillar of strength in this village. As Leeds's midwife, she's a woman who helped bring so much life into the world.

Now struck down in her own home...

...with her murderer scavenging through her bedroom.

His first mistake was killing my mother. His second was lingering for me to find him.

The soldier's startled gaze freezes on me, and the world is gone. The air is sucked out of the small, tidy room. All I see is him—wearing King John's red and gold, the tabard emblazoned with that bastard's double lion coat of arms.

But time kicks back into motion when the young soldier opens his mouth to call for reinforcements. I pull free the sword strapped to my left hip and charge him.

I level the tip of the blade at his throat. "Move, and the next death will be yours."

"You're going to kill me anyway." His panicked gaze

bounces from the length of the blade to my eyes. "Might as well try to take you with me."

I lift a single brow. "True, but not all deaths are equal. Do you want to die intact?" I glance at his crotch. "Or a eunuch?" The threat holds weight, with the sword slipping from his fingers. The clang of steel hitting smooth stone doesn't come close to the volume of the vengeance rampaging through my head. I drag in a deep breath that does nothing to calm my blinding rage. I grit my teeth and spit out, "Why Leeds?"

Because I need to hear the words, I need that confirmation.

He swallows, and the bob of his Adam's apple forces his throat to push firmer against my sword, drawing a thin line of blood along the sword's edge. "A girl," he rushes out. "Our king searches for a girl. He believes she hides here."

"Why does he want her?"

The question is, how much does John tell his men?

Again, he swallows, with the line of blood growing like a wicked red grin across his neck. Sweat beads on his forehead, following a path along the sides of his face. "I wouldn't know. I'm a soldier. I do as I'm told. Nothing more."

Without moving my weapon—or gaze—from this pathetic living corpse, I bare my teeth in a snarl. "And were your orders to slaughter my mother?"

The color drains from his face because he sees his death reflected in my eyes. "I-I was… We were told to s-spare this village if they gave us the witch or the girl."

Spare the village.

Because of my mother.

Is this John's idea of mercy? To destroy every town where there's even a rumor of a witch in his mad hunt for Rapunzel? But spare only Leeds because of his affection for my Mary Kincaid? A living saint, he once called her. And what of my father?

His life was expendable.

I give this useless piece of pig shit a cruel smile. "But they didn't give you this mysterious girl, did they?"

"No."

"No," I repeat. "Because these people know nothing about her." I lick my lips, already tasting his imminent death. I move the blade across his throat. Just enough to make him bleed a bit more. "But I do."

"Please don't kill me." His plea is pitiful.

"Did my mother beg for her life?"

He pauses for the briefest of moments. "No, she did not."

"She's a Kincaid." Of course she died with her pride preserved. "I won't allow you that dignity." I jerk my head, motioning to the floor. "On your fucking knees."

He drops like a stone next to my mother's body. "I'm sorry."

"Aye, you are."

He bows his head, with his sweat-saturated blonde hair falling over his ashen face. "I didn't have a choice."

I step toward him but keep myself out of his striking range. "Sometimes a choice is all we have, you fucking fool. Tell me, where is your king now? Where is he to protect you from me?"

"Oh, God." The coward empties his bladder. The urine leaks down his thigh to pool at his knees.

"There is no God here," I say with a bitter laugh. I use the tip of my sword to lift his chin. "There is only the son of the woman you slaughtered. Say her name. Mary Kincaid. Say it."

"M-Mary Kincaid," he stutters.

"Good boy." I tap him on the top of the head with the blade. A mock 'knighting' of him with death before bringing the sword back to his throat. "Now look at her. I want your eyes on her as you die. I want my mother to be the last thing you see in this life."

Because he was the last thing she saw.

"I did this for the king," he whispers brokenly.

"And I'm doing this for my mother." I push forward. Slow.

Twisted

Purposeful. Relish his horror as the blade slices clean through, the tip scraping against bone. "Save your almighty king a place in hell, you worthless fuck."

He gurgles on a mouthful of blood. It pulses from his neck to spill down his ugly tabard. I watch with bitter satisfaction as his life puddles at his knees. Watch until his eyes go vacant. Only when he slumps forward do I pull free the support of my weapon and allow him to fall.

Disgusted, I kick his body away from my mother lest his departing soul soil her.

I drop to my knees beside her, landing in her blood. I lift her limp, still-warm body and cradle her against my chest. Her soft brown eyes, so much like my own, stare through me, blank. Hollow. The memories of her every smile, every laugh, and every nuance of her wonderfully dynamic face are brought back to life as memories feed the ravenous fires of revenge.

To destroy the man who took everything I love from me.

To leave him as broken as he broke me.

I smooth a tangle of sticky hair from Mary Kincaid's lovely face, avoiding the slice along her throat. "I'm sorry I wasn't here to protect you."

I couldn't have done much against the king's garrison. At best, I'd have fought off a few of the soldiers before they overpowered me. Maybe that would have given my mother enough time to run. To escape into Blithe, where the witch's curse might have concealed her long enough for them to finish destroying Leeds and take their leave.

At worst, we'd have died together.

These are possibilities afforded to a fool dwelling on should haves and would haves. Gingerly, I place my fingertips on her lids and close her eyes. John came looking for Rapunzel, but he'll never find her. No one will. No one but me.

For whatever reason, I discovered her tower. Maybe Sybil indeed led me there, to Rapunzel. But it's only a matter of time before John finds Sybil. And when he does, he'll break her. It's what the bastard does. Knowing what I do about John, he'll hurt the witch until she tells him everything about Rapunzel.

By then, it won't matter.

I'll already have stolen her.

Rapunzel is mine. She's always been mine. Mine to love when we had the luxury of adolescence. Mine to punish for turning a blind eye while my father's life slipped from his body. This destruction—my mother's death—never would have happened if the selfish bitch had come away with me years ago.

Rapunzel made a choice. She hid in her precious tower while Rygard suffered for her decision.

Now she'll pay for the consequences of her choice.

~

My feet remember the way, trekking me through Blithe before my mind catches up to each step. Nothing's changed. Not in all these years. It's as if time froze in this cursed forest. Every branch still twists like broken arms protruding from the trees, pointing away from the glade. I should have heeded the silent warning when I followed that damned cloaked figure to the tower.

My mind gets turned around more than once the deeper I go, but my feet move me toward the Merrie River. I drop to the muddy bank and dip my hands in the rushing water. I scrub away my mother's blood, and the dirt of her grave caked under my fingernails. But the more I wash, the darker the stain on my soul. It takes everything I have to fight against the fury and grief dragging me down to a dangerous depth.

I stand and stretch to my full height, remembering when I was a boy and stood almost in this spot the day I found the tower. When I pretended a stick was a sword, and the future held a wealth of possibilities.

The day my life forever changed.

I clench my jaw and grind my teeth, the hot humid air a blanket wrapped around me. This forest even has a different smell than the others I traveled through. Its perfume is decay instead of life. Sybil's spell is a thick, invisible swamp as I tread lightly over the rotted remains of Peddler's Bridge.

Back on solid ground, I break into a run, batting aside gnarled branches and leaping over rotting foliage. All seem to claw at me by Sybil's hands, no doubt. The closer I get to the glade, the harder it is to focus on my intent to reach Rapunzel. I know this path by rote, but I slow my pace. Think for a moment. Do I turn left or right? All the while, my temper rises. Rage and hate bleed together, but when the tower's single silver spire comes into view, I bare my teeth in a feral snarl and forge ahead. The rest of the imposing circular structure materializes from its black roof down to each gray stone.

But I stay focused on the solitary window.

That empty window that stares out at the forest.

I stop yards away from the grim bane of my existence, a hand hovering over my sword's hilt. "Rapunzel!" My roar claps like thunder in the clearing.

I won't allow her to refuse me.

Not today.

"Rapunzel, you fucking coward, come to the window, or I swear on all that's unholy, I'll rip this tower apart with my bare hands because not stone, nor magic, nor witch can keep me from you."

But even as I issue the threat, a familiar thought slithers through my mind. One that's always nagged at me. A question I never asked because the answer was blatantly obvious, although unspoken.

How does Sybil enter the tower?

When I was a boy, I assumed the witch came and went by magic. As I grew older, I realized Sybil must have a tangible way of entering and exiting—especially given how there is a well behind the building.

Rapunzel gets her water brought to her somehow—and it's not by magical means.

Once I made that connection, I haphazardly searched the tower's base, but never with real purpose. Obviously, I overlooked Sybil's secret passage, one she likely conceals with magic.

No matter.

One way or the other, I'm gaining entry inside this goddamned tower before John's soldiers eventually find her. And they will. They're getting too fucking close. And if Rapunzel refuses to come willingly, I'll drag her out by her cursed hair.

Chapter Ten

RAPUNZEL

Wren's hatred is a spell that wraps around me, more potent than any magic Sybil could weave.

I feared he'd never return. I hoped with my whole heart he wouldn't stay away. Now he's here. I thought if Wren came back to me, we could pretend I hadn't broken his heart.

What a foolish fantasy conjured by a desperate woman seeking atonement.

One that could never become a reality.

Regret, a heavy weight on my conscience, sinks me to the floor. Wren invested everything of himself in our friendship while I held everything of myself back. He gave. I took. Because…

Because.

Because I spent my life afraid. Even during Wren's darkest moments, Sybil's warnings overrode all else. They were a deafening and constant reminder that I am a danger to myself and anyone who learned of my curse.

So I hid the truth from my only friend.

The person who opened my eyes to a world of possibilities that my cloistered life will never afford me.

Now he hates me. I despise myself, and when I slap my hands over my ears to block out Wren's shouts, I also ache to silence my conscience. I wish I could quiet the nagging voice that's haunted me during the years he was gone. The one that reminds me of what I did—what I *didn't* do. How I let his father die. That awful memory bleeds through my fingers. I fist my hands and press them harder against the sides of my head, hoping to fortify my resolve. But nothing can atone for my sin, and when I squeeze my eyes closed, Wren's visits paint themselves across my mind like precious watercolors. The stories he shared with me are bright, colorful moments I kept locked inside my mind during the grim and empty days I spent in this tower.

"Rapunzel!" At another one of Wren's ragged bellows, my eyes fly open. "Come to the goddamn window!"

I chew my bottom lip and push off the floor because I have no doubt Wren will do as he threatened. He'll find the other way into the tower.

My window to the world isn't the only access point.

Nothing is impenetrable, not even this fortress.

One more secret I kept from Wren.

The chain, fastened by a metal cuff around my ankle, is a burden as I shuffle across the room. The familiar weight slows my steps. I hitch in a trembling breath, with Wren's shouts echoing across the glade. I hang my head with guilt when I step to the open window. The fresh, summer wind whispers over me like a warning from nature.

And then my insulated world falls quiet. Deathly silent. The echo of Wren's shouts fades into the forest. I refuse to meet his glare. Then his words punch a hole through my heart. "There you are, you fucking coward."

I grip the weather-battered wooden ledge as if my life depends on it. "I'm not a coward, Wren."

"Look at me."

With effort, I lift my head. My gaze lands on a stranger who sounds like Wren. This… This striking feral creature even resembles the man who stormed away from here three years ago. They have the same dark hair. Same height. Same sharp facial features. But that's where the similarities end. This person is not the Wren I've known since I was twelve. This man has a savage and frightening edge. His hair falls to his shoulders in wild waves. His build, once lithe for hunting, is now muscular for fighting. He still carries his longbow and quiver, but he's added a broadsword, and, although I can't be sure from this distance, I think there is also a dagger at his hip.

He's dressed head to foot in muted tones of browns and greens to blend with the background, his jerkin and breeches smeared with dirt and blood. Fresh blood. It's on his face, in his hair.

Oh, God.

Has he killed someone?

Many someones?

Suddenly racked with violent tremors, I lick lips gone dry. "What do you want with me, Wren?"

"They're dead," he spits.

"Who is dead?"

"Everyone." He shoves that stubborn fall of hair away from his scowling brow. "Leeds is gone. Destroyed. Because of *you*."

"I…didn't." I step back, his accusation a physical blow. "Who would…? No. You're wrong."

No one but Sybil and Wren know I'm here. Sybil takes great pains to make sure of this. Wren is mistaken. *Please say he is mistaken.*

Wren grabs his jerkin and tugs it away from his body to angle it, giving me a better view of the blood. "Exactly. You did nothing. My mother's fucking throat was slit. Half the village still burns. All because King John wants your fucking *gift*."

My hand, on instinct, flies to my plaited hair. I never thought it was possible to be numb, cold, hot, afraid, angry, and anguished simultaneously. Yet each of those sensations collides inside of me. "That's imposs—"

"Impossible?" Wren spits out the word, his shout overlapping my hoarse denial. "My mother's blood isn't enough to convince you?" He steps forward. "This will happen one of two ways, Rapunzel. Either you tell me how to get in this fucking tower, or I'll find a way myself." His hand moves to his sword. "But I swear on God, you won't like the outcome if you don't tell me how to breach this fortress."

I'll bet everything, down to my last strand of hair, I won't like the outcome of either choice.

I collapse with a pathetic whimper. It whispers from my lips as I recall whenever Wren shared stories of Mary Kincaid, how she sang to him when he was a child. Of the treats she baked for him. How she scolded him when he arrived home muddy and soiled her freshly washed floors. Most of all, how she loved him. I ached to know a love like that for myself. Sybil tried but quickly learned she was better at protecting me than maternal affection. Although she's never been cruel, Sybil is my guardian, nothing more and nothing less.

Nothing like what Mary was to Wren.

And now Mary Kincaid is gone.

Because of me.

The bread I ate for breakfast threatens to slide up my throat on a river of bile. Somehow, I swallow it, regain my footing, and reemerge in the window. "I'm sorry."

I'm not even sure my apology carries the distance to him until Wren snarls, "No, Rapunzel." He shakes his head, the movement slow. Methodical. "You don't know what sorry is yet. But I promise you will."

The threat in Wren's tone is a blast of winter air on this summer day. Every part of me shakes, and when I open my mouth to speak, I pray I'm doing the right thing for the kingdom and myself. If King John is slaughtering my fellow Rygardians, it will do more harm than good for me to remain here.

"You won't hurt me." I say this as more of a statement than a question. The truth is, I don't know what Wren will do once the space between us is gone.

Again, he shakes his head. "Do as you're told and I won't."

His vow wraps around my throat, squeezing the breath out of me. But what motivates me into action are the innocent lives taken on my behalf.

Strangers I spent my life living in solitude to protect.

"There is a hidden access point around the back."

He points his sword at me, the blade catching the sparkle of the midday sun. "I've searched around this tower and never saw a door."

Hence, hidden. But I don't dare say this aloud and push his already fraught temper. "Trust me, Wren, it's there."

"Trust you? Never again. Trust is a commodity I can ill afford with you." Wren sheaths his weapon. "If there's no door, I'll forget my plans and let my arrow find your heart. Do we have an understanding, Rapunzel?"

I nod once. Only once because his words are busy proving me a liar twice today. We can never go back to the way things were—and I'm scared of Wren Kincaid.

Chapter Eleven

RAPUNZEL

Sybil couldn't hide me here forever.

If a boy from Leeds found me, King John will as well. It's an inevitability. When that day comes, he'll use my curse to make himself—and his army—unstoppable. Use it until there's nothing left. Until Rygard is a shadow of its current glory, and its people tremble in fear of him.

With the need to protect this kingdom at the forefront of my mind, I face Wren's hatred.

"There *is* a door at the base of the tower." I swat wisps of hair from my face. When loose, the blonde waves hit the backs of my knees. Today, however, I spent nearly an hour twisting it into a tight plait, but some strands have worked free and the breeze is blowing them into my eyes. "Go around to the back. Near the well."

"Then what? You'll toss down your braid like a rope for me to climb?"

I wince at Wren's mockery, countering with, "Or I could simply unlock the door."

"Watch your tone, Rapunzel."

He's right, of course. There's no call for sarcasm—not when

he's covered in his mother's blood. "Give me a moment to unlatch my chain."

"So much for it being unbreakable except by an enchanted blade."

"Sybil's spell holds," I insist. "She wove it in case I ever…" I let my sentence trail off and avert my eyes.

"If you ever what?" he demands.

"Tried to leave while she was gone." I drag my gaze back to him, remembering every time the loneliness threatened to drive me mad. "But Sybil has two keys. One she wears around her neck, and the other she keeps hidden inside the tower. She thinks I don't know about that one."

"Shame," Wren sneers. "I was hoping to hack off the foot."

And on that awful statement, he walks away to disappear around the back of the tower.

I don't believe he made an idle remark, and I would pledge my last breath that he would enjoy taking off my foot to get me out of this tower.

Out of this tower.

Dear God.

I'm indeed leaving. The idea doesn't seem real. Not yet, as I hurry to the stairs leading to our bedrooms on the second level, the chain scraping along behind me. I drop to my knees and remove the face of the first step to access Sybil's secret compartment. I fish out the hidden master skeleton key. It unlocks the floor panel that blocks the stairway that spirals down to the tower's secret entrance, the door, and lastly my chain.

My palms are slick, and my fingers tremble, making it nearly impossible to fit the key into the lock. But I manage. The clasp opens, and the manacle falls away. I spring to my feet and dart to the left area of the room. There, I unlock the second obstacle. A rush of cool, stale air slaps me after I lift the panel. I grab a candle to light the darkened, musty stairwell, and the moment my slippered foot touches the first step, I take a hard breath and pause, afraid. I've never moved beyond this point. My heart thunders almost painfully as I nod in silent reinforcement.

Each breath is a huff as my steps bring me closer, not toward freedom or even Wren, but an unpredictable future. And once I reach the bottom, I slide the key into the lock. I crack open the heavy door—barely an inch—when I leap back with a startled cry. The candle and key fly from my hands. The flame sputters out before hitting the floor.

Hands grab me, fisting in my yellow tunic. I'm hauled outside and slammed against the tower. Pain radiates up my spine at the impact. I blink against the blinding assault of sunlight. Against the rush of summer air that I heave into starved lungs. The woodsy aroma of the forest is so strong and too… close. It tickles my nose and makes me sneeze. I had a window to this world, but the height had dissipated its heady smells. Or is Wren's rich scent invading my senses as he fills my space? I don't know. Everything is overwhelming, and as I fight to find my footing, my feet glide over slick blades of grass.

"Stop struggling, Rapunzel." Wren's warning whips around me, his face inches from mine.

"You promised you wouldn't hurt me."

He gives me a rough shake, my back colliding with the stone again. "Behave, and I won't."

"I'm fighting because you're hurting me," I protest.

Wren releases my tunic, and I fumble for his shoulders to gain my balance. He grabs my chin and forces me to meet his angry brown eyes. I resist the urge to press into the first human touch, other than Sybil's occasional awkward embrace. "I won't tolerate disobedience from a liar like you."

Damn the tears that well in my eyes. "I never lied to you."

"No, you just withhold the whole truth." His disgust is palpable in the sliver of space between our bodies.

"It was necessary."

"That, Rapunzel, is a load of horseshit." Wren's free hand

lands with a resounding slap against the stone, so close to my head that I flinch at the impact. "This is how it will work." Wren slips his hand under my skirts. The contact with my bare flesh sends a wicked jolt of heat skidding through my body. "You're mine to punish for hiding in your precious tower when you could have stopped John from taking everything from me." He squeezes my thigh hard enough to pull a gasp from me. "First, I'll make you weep. Then, I'll make you beg. When you're good and broken—" His fingers move higher, rougher. "I'll fuck you until you can't tell the difference between pleasure and pain." He grazes along my slit, searing me through the flimsy barrier of my plain, white undergarment. "Until you won't remember a time when I wasn't inside of you."

His words are supposed to frighten me. They're supposed to disgust me—instead, my womb clenches, and desire pools between my thighs.

He kicks my legs apart and settles his large body in the space he created. The bulge of his erection digs into me when he grinds his hips against mine.

"Don't, Wren. Please. Not like this." My plea is weak and half-hearted because I want this—his hands on me. His breath on my skin. His lips on mine.

I've ached for it. Wept for it. In the dark when it was my hands between my legs.

But never like this, with hatred in his heart and venom on his lips.

There's no mercy in Wren's ruthless hands. He studies my reaction as he runs his fingers along the waistband of my underwear. His eyes, so full of animosity, miss nothing, and when he dives lower, skin on skin, I whisper out a whimper. His full lips curl in a cruel grin and he leans in so close that his warm breath fans my ear. "Calm yourself, Rapunzel. You don't get my cock today." He slides his hand lower still, his fingers parting me. Spreading me open. "That, you have to earn."

His touch is shocking. Brutal. It stokes a burning need to rock my hips against his hand to chase the brutal tease. He can't know how many nights I've done this exact thing to myself, imagining it was him. That he was with me in my bed, pleasuring me. But now he's real. Flesh and bone. Full of rage. His commanding fingers torment me with a wicked blend of pleasure and pain when they find my clit. Making slow circles over it. Flicking it. Pinching it. Owning it—*owning me.*

Soaked with need, I slick his path when he pushes a single thick finger inside me. His invasion lifts me on my tiptoes to evade the intrusion. A gasp escapes me, and I squeeze my eyes closed.

"Keep your fucking eyes open, Rapunzel. I want you looking at me."

My eyes obey before my mind rebels. His fury is frightening and thrilling as he inches in farther. He pushes deeper, stretching me wider. My lips part, with all the words I should have said years ago sitting silent on my tongue.

"That's it," he rasps. "Beg me to stop, like the coward you are."

But not *those* words.

I shake my head because it hurts so good. The delicious burn. The stretch. I never want it to end as he thrusts his finger in and out, a slow drive that knocks the breath out of me.

"I am no coward, Wren." I lean forward and feather my lips over his. He keeps his eyes open as the world melts away. *My first kiss.* But he pulls away and disappointment flays me raw. "I have sacrificed everything for Rygard." I grind against his hand. "Do your worst." Then I impale myself down to his last knuckle.

"Tempt the devil and get burned by the fires of hell." He digs up into me without mercy. Slides in a second, widening me, ripping a cry from me as he pumps them again and again. I gasp and whimper, soaking his hand. "This is only my fingers, Rapunzel. Imagine how my cock will fill you."

Twisted

Wren's words send a spark skidding across every nerve. He threatened to tear apart the tower stone by stone. Instead, he's ripping me apart thrust by thrust. Caged between the solid wall and his powerful body, I've never been a more willing prisoner. And when I rock my hips in time to the punch of his fingers, our gazes remain locked. Mine, full of wonder as new and exquisite sensations roll through me. Wren's, full of disgust as he commands me.

"Wren, please." I don't know what I need. More of everything he's already doing as he pushes my body along a sword's edge.

"Come for me, Rapunzel." There's a note of challenge in his tone and an arrogant gleam in his eyes. "Prove you're not afraid."

He repositions his hand, hitting a new spot. Rubs me just right. Slides in and out, with each punishing plunge bringing me higher. I'm lost in him—and I shatter.

Shatter into a thousand points of brilliant light. "Oh God, Wren."

Wren rewards me with one last vicious thrust of his hand, then lingers in me a moment longer as suppressed desire of the past twenty-four years drains from me. When he withdraws his fingers, I'm left empty and cold. He still has me by the wrists with my arms pinned above my head, and his face—his beautiful face—is etched with such loathing. "Tell me how it feels, Rapunzel."

I blink at his demand, my labored breaths hiccupping in my throat as I fight for a calm that's out of reach. "How *what* feels?"

"My hate," he growls. "Because that's what I gave you."

"Wren…"

Before I can say more, he yanks his hand from my underwear. Swipes fingers across my cheek, smearing a trail of wet in their wake.

He grabs hold of my right hand and lays it flat on his chest, where I find his heart pounding a frantic beat against his sternum. "Each beat feeds my need for vengeance. Against you. Against John." The king's name is poison on his tongue. "I trusted you. Loved you. And you turned your back on me. For that, I'm going to turn your entire world to rot and ruin."

Wren spits at my feet, then throws my hand away. He reaches into the pocket of his jerkin and tosses something old and crumbled at me. When I bend to pick it up, my cry echoes around us. I dart my gaze back to his face and I know in this moment I've lost him.

Lost my Wren.

The peony disintegrates against my palm as the memory of my sixteenth birthday wraps around my heart to squeeze so tightly that I can barely breathe.

I'll give it to you on the day you leave this tower.

That was Wren's promise, and he's held on to this decayed flower for eight years.

Oh, God.

I think of running for one fleeting moment because there will be no reprieve from Wren's wrath. As he's said, I'm as guilty as the king, and nothing I say will change his mind.

But Wren must read my intentions because a sneer twists his lips. "I dare you. Run, Rapunzel. The chase may grant you temporary freedom, but the scars I'll leave on your body will last a lifetime." He strides away. "You best keep pace."

Keep pace? I can't even breathe, much less *walk* after his brutal touch. But somehow, I put one foot in front of the other and hurry to match his long, hurried gait as we cross the glade. I use the sleeve of my tunic to wipe my cheek raw, ridding myself of the physical evidence of Wren's vengeance. Wishing I could somehow scrub it from my soul as well.

I hold back tears and muster the remaining shreds of my tattered dignity. "Where are you taking me?"

His large hand wraps around my wrist like a manacle. "Away from here."

Obviously.

I dig my heels in the pliable dirt at the tree line, and for the briefest moment, I marvel at how the ground gives at the pressure. I've known only relentless stone and grim grays. For a breath of time, I'm...overwhelmed...at the things I've seen only from my window. Never have I felt so small. So insignificant, and when I spin and see the tower, I gape in horror at the stark monstrosity.

Wren releases my wrist, and the lost momentum causes me to trip and fall to my knees. I slap my hands over my mouth to muffle my cry as I gaze in appalling wonder at my home.

My prison.

My sanctuary.

How have I never realized how tall and ugly it is?

Because I was on the inside looking out.

"Wren." His name seeps from between my fingers. He crouches in front of me and pries my hands from my face. His broad frame blocks the tower from my view. I focus on beautiful him because even after what he did to me and whatever he's about to do, I can't deny my connection to him—and affection for him. And I hate myself for it. "I'm scared."

I also hate myself for admitting this truth.

"As was my mother." His hands squeeze around my wrists as he yanks me to my feet. His black brows are angry slashes above fierce eyes. "Be grateful I don't show you the same *mercy* John's soldier showed her."

And then we're moving again, treading into a forest I've seen only from my window. I have no time to absorb any of its ominous splendor. Not when I have all to do to keep up with Wren's furious pace. He jerks my arm, tugging me along, causing me to stumble over the twigs and branches that litter the forest floor. Animals scurry out of sight as we weave around gnarled trees. Birds fly high overhead, disappearing into the canopy of leaves. I gape in wonder, having read about these creatures in books. They are as fantastical to me—as mythical—as dragons and unicorns. I gape at the world around me, with everything too...close.

Too *real*.

The air is too hot and heavy.

The muted sounds of the forest whisper as loud as thunder.

The intoxicating woodsy aroma overwhelms my senses.

And Wren.

He is everywhere. A riot around me. His hand a clamp around my arm. His hatred wrapped around my heart, making each beat a torment. What he did to me against the tower still sings through my veins. All of it too much too soon.

Pulling me apart.

When I slide a glance at him, I'm struck by his height. I never realized how tall he stands. How could I? It was impossible to accurately gauge his stature. The top of my head barely reached his chin when he had me pinned against the tower. His hair, which I thought was black, is actually shot through with sun-kissed strands of brown. And his face. He's always been handsome, even as a boy. But this version of him?

He is...terrifyingly beautiful.

It's his eyes. Those intense brown eyes, so full of rage. They harbor death. Maybe mine, I ponder when we reach the river. Wren bypasses a bridge, dragging me farther down to one that—

No. There is no way I'm crossing those rotten and broken wooden boards. I'm sure his intentions are for me to meet my demise right here, right now, by letting me drown.

"Are you mad?" I point to the remnants of what must have once been a sturdy means across the Merrie River.

Wren gives me a vicious smile. "I thought I cleared up any confusion about my state of mind when I finger-fucked you against your precious tower."

The tower has never been precious to me. "This will never support our weight."

He releases my wrist with a little shove that propels me onto the rickety bridge. "Walk, Rapunzel."

With no choice but to comply, I grip the prickly, frayed rope, barely holding the bridge together. I take the first few steps. The bridge groans and sways, and I freeze in horror, expecting the decayed boards to splinter beneath my feet. But Wren is directly behind me. He curls his hand around the nape of my neck, squeezing.

His breath is warm against my ear. "Did I tell you to stop?"

"I'm afraid."

His nasty laugh hurts worse than a slap. "Good. Now fucking walk, or I'll drag you across this bridge by your goddamn hair."

The venom in Wren's tone pollutes the air when he releases me. His threat propels me forward across the bridge. I almost hope the boards will crumble and I'll fall into the rushing water below just to spite him. To rob him of the pleasure of killing me himself. I shuffle one foot in front of the other, my yellow tunic catching in the summer breeze to tangle around my trembling legs all the way until I reach the other side. Then he's there beside me, with another warning for me to keep up with his punishing pace.

Or else.

To me, Blithe Forest always seemed large. A vast expanse that stretched on forever. With their twisted branches, the tall trees block out the rest of Rygard. However, it's much smaller than I thought. We walk for less than an hour in silence, which allows me to lay my starved and greedy gaze on the world. To enjoy the glory of seeing something other than the same stone walls. The same…everything. But the silence becomes too thick between us, and I finally work up the courage to, again, ask Wren where he's taking me.

Without missing a step, he answers, "Where you belong. Hell."

I can't imagine how much worse my life can get, given that I spent twenty-four miserable years in a cage, often half-mad from solitude. But I get a good idea when, a moment later, we reach the edge of the forest, and there, perched upon two massive steeds, are our escorts to the underworld—one with eyes as black as a demon's.

Chapter Twelve

WREN

Loyalty is everything.
 Without loyalty, there is no trust. Without trust, there are only lies, betrayal, and bloodshed. John proved this by infecting Rygard with his cleverly concealed evil and demented desire to possess Rapunzel. And Rapunzel reinforced this by hiding her gift from me.

Me.

Someone who would have given his life to protect her.

I was a fool in love with an illusion. A person I crafted in my mind because I never knew the person beneath the fantasy I created.

But Dax and Quinn, they've proved their loyalty to me—and I to them. So much so, I trusted them with the knowledge of Rapunzel—Rapunzel and her fucking magical ability to heal.

I can't even look at her as we journey southwest, away from Blithe. Away from the charred remains of Leeds. Putting as much distance as possible between me and my mother's grave before the sun sets and we stop for the night.

I need to put an end to this vile day.

Speaking of vile things…

Rapunzel, hidden from view by Dax's brawny body, hasn't complained once. Yet. Surprising given how we've been traveling for hours, and she was initially reluctant to ride with Dax. Her protest was absurd. Every woman he meets falls at his feet. Yet there she was, refusing to climb on the saddle and take a seat in front of him. Regardless, I hoisted her up, and she's been sitting there, stiff as wood since.

Before we started our trek toward Dyhurst, I changed out of my soiled jerkin and replace it with a clean garment. Somehow, though, I still feel saturated in Mary Kincaid's blood. My sorrow is there, simmering beneath the surface, but there's no time to grieve. Not until John is dead and Rygard is free. Instead, there is rage, and when I gaze out at the landscape, at Rygard's undeniable beauty, it reinforces the need to rid this land of its maniacal king.

Realizing I'm gripping Frenzy's reins tight enough to slow the black steed's pace, I loosen my hold and quicken the animal's gait. Riding parallel to Dax, I glimpse Rapunzel, and lust, pure and hot, fills my cock, hardening it to the point of pain. Fuck. I can still feel her, tight and wet around my fingers.

I wanted to hurt her, wanted her shame.

She gave me her passion.

Goddamn her.

"I see Felkirk village," Quinn announces from his vantage point a few yards ahead of us.

Although I wish my friend hadn't surrendered his soul, Quinn's decision has certain advantages. He sees farther and sharper than the average mortal. Hears a whisper like a roar. He's also stronger. Faster. His body withstands fatal injuries with unnatural ease.

But the demon left something else behind as well. Something dark. Sinister. Something Quinn has called upon only once, and when he did, it required all of his strength and left him weakened for days afterward. A malevolent force with the power to rip the life clean out of a person's body.

Frowning, I crane my neck and squint against the sun's glare. In the distance, barely a smudge on the horizon, is Felkirk's distinct palisade. "You'd think, by now, they'd have replaced their primitive defensive wall with one of stone." I remember coming here as a boy. They're notoriously cautious of strangers, as they should be in these chaotic times. But my father supplied the village with meat for years, so I'm familiar with this place well enough. "For the right price, they'll welcome us."

Ancient and small, Felkirk was always forgettable in John's mind. That makes it the ideal haven for us to enjoy a hot meal and sleep in a soft bed for the night.

Quinn shoots Rapunzel a glare before jerking his head to a dense, distant forest south of Felkirk. "It would be better to make camp in those woods."

"I volunteer to share my pallet with Rapunzel," Dax offers. "Seeing as we're riding companions, it seems only right." He rubs his cheek on her hair, eyes closed, as if in a state of ecstasy. When he reopens them, he hunches over her so she can get a good look at his devious grin. "What say you, Little Captive, you want to spend the night in my arms?"

Although I can't see Rapunzel's face, I notice how she stiffens at the idea. Dax's bemused expression is comical. He's unaccustomed to women finding his advances unwelcome. I don't blame them for their enthusiasm after sharing close quarters with the man. We've fucked different women in the same room together.

Women appreciate Dax's playfulness.

Some women enjoy Quinn's penchant for pain.

I get the job done well enough, with each female face a blur and every body the wrong one—because it wasn't *hers*.

I should have fucked Rapunzel right there, against the tower. Tossed up her skirts and had done with it to finally rid myself of this hunger for her. I intended to turn her body into an instrument of torture against itself. Push her to the threshold of ecstasy, then leave her empty and wanting. Same as she left me all those times I begged her to run away with me. But once I started touching her, I couldn't stop—and in the process, I tortured myself.

"I'm fine with whatever you decide." Rapunzel's voice is a husky whisper. But then she adds louder, "Although anonymity would be a wiser choice."

Rapunzel's green eyes are locked on me, and although her tone may be docile, her gaze is challenging.

"We bed down in Felkirk," I grit out between clenched teeth, if for no other reason than to be contrary. Because sometimes sound judgment is blind when pride is involved.

"Wren—"

"Was I unclear?" I snap at Quinn.

Quinn flares his nostrils, and his mouth compresses to an angry line. He kicks his black steed into a gallop and rides ahead, his way of letting me know I'll have to deal with his temper later. As for Dax...

"Objections?" I demand.

Dax shrugs and shakes his head. "None I'm willing to voice."

"Smart man." I whip my gaze at Rapunzel. She shakes her head in silent rebuff. "You have something to say?"

She drags the tip of her tongue across her lips. "No, Wren, I don't. You seem to have it all worked out in your mind."

She settles against Dax's chest, and he bends to whisper in her ear. Something I can't hear. Something intimate that curls her pink lips in a ghost of a grin. Their private exchange shouldn't irritate me. I shouldn't be jealous.

And I'm not.

Dax and Quinn are part of the plan to break Rapunzel.

Being soulless, Quinn was easier to convince. Dax took a little longer to persuade, but not by much because he does like shiny new toys. I may hate her, but there's no denying Rapunzel is exquisite. Tiny. Delicate. Emotionally starved after a lifetime of captivity.

She'll break easily beneath our hands.

Then I'll dump her used body like trash at the feet of our almighty king—right before I murder that motherfucker for ordering my parents' death.

Because fuck her. She means nothing to me.

And if I keep telling myself this lie, I might actually will it into reality.

∼

Quinn, the ornery bastard, hangs back with Dax and Rapunzel while I have a brief exchange with Felkirk's gatekeeper. He allows us inside after fleecing us of more shillings than I intended to part with to gain entry. But it's money well spent. Here, the people keep to themselves. They're less likely to have heard the rumors about Rapunzel. We're safe for the night, at the very least. Come dawn, we'll be back on the road, on our way to the abandoned castle we've called home for the past year. But it'll take over a day of hard riding to reach Dyhurst.

We stable our horses at the village green and drape Rapunzel in a drab brown cloak. Quinn yanks the hood over her head and tries to get as much of her hair tucked beneath it as possible. We stroll the short distance to the White Horse Inn, blending with the handful of people milling about the antiquated village.

We claim a cozy table in the back of the inn's main room and sit Rapunzel between Dax and Quinn, facing the wall. I'm across from them, my eyes on the crowd. She keeps the hood drawn but peeks around it at the assortment of locals gathered in this small space. A fire burns in a huge stone hearth where a roasting pig flavors the smokey air.

A server rushes over with tankards of ale. "Hail and well met, good sirs and milady." Her smile reveals deep dimples as she sets the four cups on the table. "Will you be dining with us this evening?"

"Aye," Dax confirms. "And rooms as well."

"Yes, of course, but there's only one room available for the night." Her gaze lingers on Rapunzel, who peeks back at her from beneath the cloak's hood.

Quinn lifts a single brow, his black eyes cold. "That won't be a problem."

If she's scandalized by our acceptance of the sleeping arrangement—or by Quinn's soulless eyes—she wisely keeps it to herself. "Of course. I'll bring four plates."

Then she's off, weaving around the empty tables. No one pays us any mind, although we make sure Rapunzel keeps the damn hood in place to hide her golden fucking hair.

"We'll leave at dawn and ride hard until we reach the Soren River. That should get us as far as Davenport," I calculate.

Dax is already nodding, his blonde shaggy hair a mess after a relentless day of riding. "Aye, but we'll need to be mindful of where we make camp."

"That's Grayson territory." Quinn slides a glare at Wren and shakes his head, clearly annoyed. "Still say I should have killed Edward when I had the chance."

I roll my eyes at Quinn's complaint. "Back then, you were still too quick with your sword."

"But I'm so good at spilling blood." Then Quinn looks pointedly at Rapunzel. "And now you get to have your fun, while we had to restrain ourselves when it was our turn. How convenient."

"Edward didn't wrong you. He annoyed you. There is a difference." My temper rises at the memory of my father dying over six brutally long days and the vision of my mother's body bleeding out on her chamber floor.

Twisted

"I didn't wrong you." Rapunzel's audacity is a slap to my face.

I lean forward, getting as close to her as the table allows. "Then why the fuck are your eyes filled with guilt?"

"You see what you want to see, Wren." She drops her head to stare at her lap, and when she does, Dax drapes an arm around her shoulder. He opens his mouth to speak, to calm the growing tension between us, no doubt, but silences himself when the server returns, balancing four heaping plates of food.

She places the heaping plates on the table, then wipes her hands on the food-stained apron tied around her trim waist. "May I get you anything else?"

Just then, a burly man with a bushy gray beard sitting a few tables away bellows, "Joan, get your sweet self over here with another jug of ale."

"We're good." Quinn slides a dangerous glare at the man.

She bobs a quick curtsy. "Shout if you need me."

The moment she turns her back, Dax, Quinn, and I dig into our food. After consuming only bread and the occasional apple for days, a hearty meal is most welcome. Rapunzel, however, picks at her plate.

Quinn notices and bumps her with his shoulder. "Problem, Princess? Meal too primitive for your standards?"

"It's delicious, actually." She slips a piece of the roasted pig between her lips. Chews, swallows, then gives Quinn a hesitant look. "I'm…overwhelmed."

I throw her a smirk. "I'd tell you to relax, that we're going to take care of you, but unlike you, I'm not one for duplicity."

Clearly miserable, she shoves her plate away.

Quinn stabs his knife in the meat and, without missing a beat, pulls the dish toward him. "Shame to let food rot."

After finishing our meal and a second serving of ale, we weave our way through the subdued crowd and head up the stairs that lead to the sleeping quarters.

A single bed built for two sits ominously in the center of the sparse room. There's a full basin of water resting atop a utilitarian cabinet. A small, weathered table with two rickety chairs, and a chamber pot make up the rest of the contents of our quarters.

Dax insists we give the bed to Rapunzel, whereas I don't give a fuck if she sleeps outside with the livestock. But I relent because I'm exhausted and in no mood to argue. While Quinn builds a fire in the hearth, I splash water on my face before unrolling my pallet.

While we were downstairs, rain came and brought with it bone-chilling dampness. Listening to the storm pelting Felkirk, I glance at Rapunzel, who hides in a corner trying to make herself invisible. Dust from the road mutes the yellow of her tunic, but nothing can dull the golden glow of her fucking hair. She sways on her feet, and the dark circles under her eyes show that she's about to drop. When she shifts from foot to foot before crossing her legs, I realize she hasn't asked to relieve herself in hours.

"Rapunzel."

Her eyes go wide, and her frantic gaze shoots to me. "What now, Wren?"

I jerk my head at the chamber pot in the far corner. "Use it before you piss yourself."

Horrified, she glares at me as if I've gone mad. "I wouldn't dare with the three of you in the room."

"Fucking womanly airs," Quinn grumbles.

Dax, much to my annoyance, comes to her rescue. "How about, just for tonight, we ease her into your torture plan, eh?" He herds us toward the door. "Let's give Rapunzel a moment of privacy to do her business. Wren, you have my leave to go back to snarling at her after she's finished."

Before I can agree or stop him from ushering us out of the cramped room, I'm one of three fools standing in the hallway waiting on Rapunzel to finish whatever the hell she's doing in the room. Intentionally or not, Dax will sabotage the severity of my retribution against her. And maybe that's why I brought them along. He and Quinn will stop me from going too far and losing the fragile grip I still have on my humanity. Because they know what I've become after I learned the depth of John's evil.

I became a monster to kill the devil who wears the crown.

Chapter Thirteen

DAX

I've engaged in many intimate acts with countless women over the years. Sleeping, however, was never one of them.

Waking up next to Rapunzel, I must admit, is not unpleasant. Her curves mold nicely in all my grooves. We're a perfect fit, and it makes it painfully difficult not to peel away the barrier of our clothing and sink into her warmth. Especially with her wiggling her delectable backside against my groin every time she languidly shifts in her sleep.

Good Lord, the woman could tempt a saint—and I'm far from pious.

In fact, I'm downright depraved.

Wren gave us leave to use Rapunzel at our leisure. Currently, with her snuggled against me, I might have to make good on his generous offer. Especially when she stretches, and her entire length glides over me.

Her breathing speeds, and her tiny body stiffens, alerting me she's transitioned from a peaceful slumber to wakefulness. And then she stops breathing altogether at the realization that although she went to bed alone, she certainly hasn't woken up that way.

Twisted

"What are you doing in this bed?" Rapunzel's groggy demand is adorable.

"Sleeping until someone roused me by rubbing her ass along my cock," I practically purr as I wrap an arm around her and drag her back to me when she tries to squirm away.

"You can't be here."

"My shillings that paid for this room say I can." Am I bullying her? Absolutely. Do I care? Not at all.

She looked too inviting, curled under the blanket last night. Too enticing now not to tease.

Again, she attempts to scramble away, then squeaks when my arm tightens around her. "You were supposed to stay on the floor."

"Let me tell you a secret, Rapunzel," I whisper. "I never do as I'm told."

The rising sun filtering through the wooden slats covering the window turns Rapunzel's hair to golden flames when she cranes her neck to peer at Wren and Quinn. They're still on their pallets by the dying fire. She flops back down, a scowl marring her lovely face. "They stayed put."

"They must not have gotten cold during the night." I trail my hand over her hip and smirk at her sharp intake of breath. "I did."

Forgive me, Father, for I am a liar.

Truth is, Rapunzel spent the day bouncing on my horse. It made me wonder what it would feel like to have her bounce on my cock during the night.

Wren claims to hate her. I'd bet my last breath that's why he kept his stubborn ass on the floor when all he's wanted since he was a boy was to get this woman in his arms. I don't believe for a moment he actually detests her. He's simply nurturing a severe fit of anger—which is righteous, of course, but in my opinion misdirected.

And Quinn, well, he's a miserable prick on a good day. To

him, women are good for one thing—and it doesn't involve getting cozy.

"You could have added more wood to the fire."

"Or you could take off your clothes and cuddle with me." I roll her a bit, enough to give me better access to the front of her body. I trail my hand to her stomach and find it amusing how she stiffens beneath my touch. "This is the heat I want." I dance my fingers lower and gather her skirts. When I drag the material up her legs, she releases the sweetest and weakest whimper in protest. "No need to be shy. Wren told us you let him finger-fuck you against the tower."

Rapunzel molds herself against me, as if to escape from my hand—in the wrong direction, I might add. All she does is give me better access. It's obvious she's starved for contact. Given what else Wren told us, she spent much of her life alone. If I were her, I'd be screaming for someone to touch me, too.

"I didn't let him."

"But you didn't want him to stop, either." It's not a question. "Just like you don't want me to stop now."

"I *do* want you to stop."

I nuzzle her hair, marveling at its softness against my cheek. It's strange to know that within this tiny woman is a power so great, John is destroying his own kingdom to find her.

But right now, in my arms, body pressed to mine and green eyes wide with wonder, she's no enchanted creature. Rapunzel is a woman full of curiosity after a lonely lifetime trapped in solitude. And unlike Wren, I'm not holding a grudge against her. I may be a thief and murderer, but I have a tender spot for the fairer sex.

Speaking of sex…

I skate my palm along her delicate flesh, loving how her soft curves are a contrast to my hard angles. "I see the lie written in your eyes." Gooseflesh chases the path of my hand when I inch higher. Her resistance weakens as I coax her legs apart and tease her inner thigh. She makes such sweets sounds when I cup her cunt. "Tell me, Rapunzel, what did it feel like to have Wren's fingers inside you?"

She hesitates, but only for a moment. "Scandalous." Then confesses in a breathy hush, "But also thrilling."

"Good girl." I reward her honesty with the slide of my finger along the seam of her pussy. The damp material between us is irritating. I ache for flesh on flesh. "Let's remove these cumbersome undergarments, shall we?"

"No, Dax, please." She struggles to close her legs.

Then she gasps when she sees Quinn at the foot of the bed. His disheveled, shoulder-length black hair and scar-ravaged body add to the theatrics of his scowl. A muscle tics in his clenched jaw as he watches us with abysmal eyes. He heaves in a deep breath and then, without warning, jerks away the scratchy blanket.

Rapunzel scrambles, making a valiant grab for the cover. For a large man, Quinn is quicker than a miser running from the tax collector. The cloth sails across the room, leaving Quinn a daunting figure in nothing but his breeches. He looms beside the bed with hands on his hips and nostrils flared with anticipation. The vine-like markings that adorn his bare chest seem to twist and stretch across his torso under the glow of the dying, flickering fire.

In a tangle of hair, Rapunzel tries to yank down her skirt. But Quinn is determined. He shoves his large, tattooed hands under her skirts and, despite her protests, tugs off her underwear in a single rough pull. There's the rending of fabric when he rips them from her body. She slaps at his hands. Struggles to scurry off the bed, but I grab her and slam her back against my chest.

"Easy," I soothe. "We won't hurt you. Quinn won't even touch you." I use the wall to prop myself upright, facing her toward Quinn. With one arm wrapped around her torso, I guide her leg over mine, spreading her. "It will just be me. Do you want that, Rapunzel? Do you want my hands on you?"

She's trembling, and her heart is beating a frantic rhythm as she stares at Quinn. And he's watching her, his face shrouded in shadow with eyes like two dark hollows. "Yes." Her husky confession is so soft, I barely hear it. "But I'm afraid."

"Of me? No, Little Captive. I don't enjoy pain with my pleasure." Smirking, I flick my gaze at my soulless friend. "That's Quinn's game. For me, it's all about the fun. Now, off this comes. We need to see you properly."

Again, Rapunzel hesitates, and I allow her the few precious moments she needs to gather her courage. While I wait in blessed agony, the tension eases out of her. Once she's ready, I lift first the yellow tunic over her head, then the white chemise. I toss both gowns aside—aiming them at Wren. Then I take a moment to look my fill of her because, my God, this woman is exquisite.

Rapunzel's hair is a golden curtain around her, pooling on the linen-covered straw mattress. Her chin is high in a brave display of dignity, with a captivating mix of curiosity and trepidation in her striking green eyes.

Quinn, who isn't a man affected by much, sucks in a hard breath as he drinks in the sight of her. And, stubbornly on his pallet, Wren sits up straighter for a better view.

Can't blame them.

Every part of Rapunzel is flawless. All smooth, pale flesh with dusty-rose-tipped breasts that beg to be sucked. A glimpse between her legs has me wondering if the brown curls are as soft as they look. The need for the tight squeeze of her cunt around my cock is all-consuming, and when she crosses her arms over her chest, I grab them and hold them wide.

With a shake of my head, I *tsk* her. "Absolutely not, Rapunzel. To conceal such beauty is a sin."

I didn't think it possible for her cheeks to flame redder. I was wrong. "Please. I'm so embarrassed."

"Of perfection?" I honestly wonder if her years of isolation have addled her wits.

She glances at Quinn, avoiding Wren entirely. "This is…unseemly."

I place a kiss on her brow before pressing her down on the mattress. "Your view of the situation is askew." I feather my lips around the shell of her ear. "There is nothing shameful happening here. You dreamed of this, haven't you? During those lonely years in the tower. My God, Rapunzel. Let me worship every inch of your body."

A tear slips from the outer corner of her eye. It disappears in her hair, that's fanned out in a golden halo around her head. "Please…" she breathes.

"You beg so pretty." I brush my lips over hers, my dick hard as stone knowing Quinn is watching us. I'm a shameless exhibitionist. Unfortunately, Rapunzel is having a bit of trouble relaxing under his watchful eye. She's stiff beneath me, breaking away from my mouth to again glance at Quinn. I grab her chin and force her to focus on me. "Ignore him. Right now, it's all about you and me, Little Captive."

She blinks her beautiful green eyes, and in them is a clash of trepidation and awe. I dive back in at her tentative nod, kissing her until her slender arms snake around my torso. She grabs my shirt, her fingers twining in the worn, white material. Twisting it and pulling at it as I devour her mouth. But this isn't where I want to be. Not when there's so much more of her to explore. I kiss along the line of her jaw, then work my way to the delicate column of her throat, where I press my lips to the frenzied pulse under her ear. At the shock of my teeth, she lets out a little cry when I nip the sensitive flesh.

Still not satisfied, I move lower to her pert breasts. I take one pebbled peak in my mouth. Above us, Quinn's primal growl resonates throughout the room. Rapunzel arches her back, pressing into me, silently offering herself. I suck and tug, graze her nipple with my teeth to pull a gasp from her. What an enchanting sound. So lovely, I need to hear it again.

And again, and again.

When the bed dips from the weight of Quinn's knee, I keep her concentrated on what I'm doing rather than on him. But Quinn, a man not easily ignored, clamps one hand around her throat to nail her in place. His other hand frees his cock from the confines of his breeches. All the while, he keeps his gaze fixed on me as I lick my way to her flat, taut stomach.

Rapunzel struggles under Quinn's hold, straining against the pressure of his grip. "Let me go."

"You'll stay as you are."

She tries to pry away his hand. "You promised he wouldn't touch me."

I stroke the soft brown curls between her legs, curious about why they don't match the hair on her head. Yesterday, I also noticed small sections of short brown strands interwoven in the silken golden mass, but right now, I spend only a fleeting moment pondering this oddity. Not with my face this close to the juncture of her incredible thighs.

"Did I?" I give her a naughty grin. "Allow yourself to enjoy this, Rapunzel. Go easy. Let us enjoy you. Show us how beautiful you are when you submit."

Quinn must have eased his hold on her throat because she turns her head and watches as he slides his palm over his engorged shaft. The tip of her tongue peeks out to run along her plump bottom lip, wordlessly speaking of desire, not timidity. She swallows hard, her chest rising and falling with each frantic breath she takes.

"The day will come when you'll beg me to fuck you," Quinn growls in her ear.

Then he shocks her—and me—by savaging her mouth.

There's no other way to describe how he forces her jaw open to sweep his tongue inside. He swallows her whimper and answers back with a groan. For a man who isn't fond of kissing, he's doing a magnificent job of proving to be quite adept at the task. If I weren't having my fun teasing Rapunzel, I'd give him a rousing round of applause—the consequence of his wrath at my teasing be damned.

Quinn pumps his cock while I glide my lips over her flesh, past her navel to her cunt. When I skate my tongue up her slit, Rapunzel moans into Quinn's mouth and practically shoots off the bed. I wrap my arms under and around her thighs to hold her where I need her. Part her lips with my thumbs, and dive into her. Mouth-fuck her until she's writhing on the mattress. Her fingers dig into my hair as she pushes my head closer. Rocks her hips in time with the thrusts of my tongue.

Can't say there isn't a certain thrill derived from knowing no other man has touched Rapunzel so intimately. Wren may have had his fingers here, but I'm the first to have my face between her legs. The first to sample her delicious pussy. I briefly pull away to glance over my shoulder at Wren and see his body has betrayed him.

He can fool Rapunzel, but Wren can't fool Quinn and me. His labored breathing and his fixed attention on us have me jerking my head in invitation. The stubborn prick responds with a snarling silent no. So be it. If he doesn't want to join, or even have a better view, that's on him.

I dive back on Rapunzel's clit with a hard suck. She breaks away from Quinn's kiss to breathe my name. To my utter shock, she removes a hand from my hair to slide it around Quinn's arm. She's voluntarily touching him. It's an honest to God miracle. And what's even more startling...he lets her. This *is* Quinn, after all. But he's allowing her to hold on to him as I lick and nip at her. All the while, he strokes his cock, his feral growls mingling with Rapunzel's soft whimpers.

My dick is so hard it aches. With Rapunzel lost in the moment, I no longer have to hold her legs open. I fit comfortably between her thighs, with a pressure building in my shaft that aches to the point of agony. Never have my balls tightened to pain, but here we are. I lift my hips to free my cock and massage my shaft. Each grind against my palm is nothing short of euphoric.

Quinn releases Rapunzel's throat, and it takes a few more tugs on his long, thick cock to find his release. He breaks the kiss and comes on her perfect breasts with a guttural roar that resonates throughout the small room. Then, like the savage he is, he smears two fingers in his mess and puts them to her swollen lips.

"This is yours, Rapunzel." He presses his slick fingers to her parted lips. "Clean them."

Her studious tongue darts out to lave Quinn's fingers. He pushes them deep into her mouth, and the sight of her sucking on them sends me over the edge.

I pull her to the edge of the bed and kneel between her legs. Slide a finger in her dripping pussy, with Rapunzel's moan filling the room like music. I pump in and out of her, fucking her gently as I work her clit with my mouth. My other hand glides up my shaft, and I use the precum to ease my strokes, squeezing, bringing myself so close. Too close. But I hold back. Delay the pleasure. Torturing myself.

"Next time, I'm fucking your mouth," Quinn warns her, dropping his foot on the floor and straightening to his full height. "Do you see what you are doing to Wren? He aches to fuck you as badly as Dax and I do. How does that make you feel, Rapunzel?"

She arches her back and bears down against my mouth. "It pleases me."

"Even though he claims to hate you?" Quinn is ruthless as he tugs up his breeches.

Twisted

"Yes," she breathes. "Because I don't hate him back."

Behind me, Wren groans long and low. I want to glance behind me to see if it's because he's close to coming or because of her confession, but I'll be damned if I'll pull my mouth from Rapunzel to find out.

"You've been such a good girl." Quinn rubs his cum over her nipples and then blows on them, making them tighten. Rolls the tormented peaks between his fingers. Pinches them hard enough to make her cry out. Introduces Rapunzel to pleasure with pain. "Now come for us."

Her legs stiffen, then tremble. Every muscle in her body strains as she chases her release. Keep working her and drink the rush of ecstasy that floods my mouth when she finds it. I pump my cock faster. Harder. Squeeze tighter. Imagine what my cock will feel like wrapped inside her wet warmth.

That's the push I need to find my release. I pinch my eyes closed and shoot thick ropes of cum into my hand, wishing it was her cunt. Savoring the remnants of her climax on my tongue, I pull my head from Rapunzel's legs and wipe my mouth with the back of my hand. Quinn is standing over her with a wicked grin as sharp as the scar on his face. Rapunzel is sweaty and heaving, hair wild around her. A glance at Wren shows him tucking his spent cock in his breeches. He pushes himself to his feet, his upper lip curled in a snarl. He probably doesn't know whether to hate her or himself at this moment.

With my clean hand, I retrieve the blanket from the floor and toss it at Rapunzel. The arrogant prick I am, I keep my breeches down as I cross the room to the basin and use the tepid water to wash.

"That was interesting." I offer Rapunzel a mischievous wink. "I've never had my tongue inside a lady before. Women, yes, but never an actual lady."

"She's no fucking lady." Wren whips back at me.

I roll my eyes as I clean my cock. "She's still on my tongue, and I'm telling you, that's the taste of a lady. You're just grumpy because it wasn't your mouth she poured into."

"We should have left you on the road, your deflated cock flapping against your balls, with Lord Nolan chasing after you," Wren grumbles.

Releasing a false, wounded gasp, I slap a hand over my heart. "Such cruelty."

Wren stabs a finger at Rapunzel. "You have less than an hour to get yourself together before we take to the road."

Rapunzel, her hair a riot of golden waves, clutches the blanket to her breast. She nods, her eyes flooded with unshed tears.

To soften Wren's brutality, I say to her, "Little Captive, you wash, and I'll procure you a fresh gown."

Her watery smile is devastating. "Thank you."

"See?" I motion to her, but I address Wren and Quinn. "Gratitude. It's nice to have someone who finally appreciates—"

"One more word, and I'll slit your fucking throat."

"Fear not," I assure Rapunzel. "Wren is more bluster than bite. He won't kill me."

At least, I hope he won't. John's order to raze Leeds and the subsequent murder of Mary Kincaid has, in a single day, changed Wren for the worse. For as long as I've known him, he's been cold and measured, whereas Quinn is hot and aggressive. Now, his temper has an unpredictable edge, which is dangerous for all of us.

"I would hope not," she whispers. "The innkeeper might charge extra to scrub the room."

It takes me a moment to grasp Rapunzel's jest. When I do, I let out a hearty laugh. "Wren, she's not as meek as you thought."

Rapunzel tilts her head, regarding me with avid curiosity. "You assumed I was meek?"

I motion to Wren. "He did."

"Well, Wren is wrong." She notches her chin. "There were

two paths I could have taken while locked in the tower, one of madness and one of fortitude. Guess which one I chose."

Quinn strides up to her, gathers a fistful of her hair at the nape, and tugs her head back. "A wise woman knows her place."

Rapunzel narrows her eyes on him, and a hint of a smile curves her lips. "And where will you place me?" She waves a hand at the straw mattress beneath her. "In a bed? Or on top of your…" She motions at his cock. "A woman's place is at a man's side. A wise man would keep her there lest she walk behind him with a clear view of his back. It gets her to thinking of all the ways she can take advantage of her position to put a blade between his—"

"She's going to be trouble," Quinn cuts her off, then glares at her for a good long while before releasing her with a jerk.

Wren drags a hand through his dark, rumpled hair. "She'll do as she's told."

I bounce my gaze from Wren to Quinn to Rapunzel and know, without a doubt, one thing is for certain—now that she's free, she won't comply with petty demands.

Once we reach Dyhurst, it will be entertaining to watch Wren try to maintain his ridiculous hatred for Rapunzel given the raw desire that burns in his eyes whenever he looks at her. Wren may have freed her from the tower, but he's trapped them both in a mental prison he constructed the day his father died. When he rids himself of that rage and finds peace, he'll realize that Rapunzel isn't to blame for his pain.

Then they'll be free—if he doesn't kill them both first.

Chapter Fourteen

RAPUNZEL

Everything hurts. Muscles I never knew I had ache from hours spent in the saddle. Not to mention my…lady parts…feel wholly abused. Also, my bladder is ready to burst. However, I would rather rip out my tongue than voice a single complaint. Not even to Dax, who proved he's the kinder of my three companions after this morning.

'Captors' is a more fitting term.

Companions. Captors. No matter.

I'm free from the oppressive walls. No cumbersome chain to tether me to my prison during Sybil's long absences. Surrounded by open space and fresh air, I'm afraid this is a wondrous dream. One I'll wake from to find Sybil standing over my bed and the musty tower air choking the life from me one breath at a time.

Wren claims he's taking me to hell. I'll suffer the consequences of whatever future awaits me rather than a lifetime spent in a stone cage now that I've sampled freedom.

Now that I've felt pleasure from someone else's touch.

I never realized how much I yearned for human contact until I woke this morning in a new bed, wrapped in a man's arms.

Twisted

It was a promising start to this day.

Self-preservation and propriety dictate I should have put up a fight. That I shouldn't have allowed Dax and Quinn to take such liberties with my body. But it felt too good to be adored —if only for those precious moments. All my inhibitions melted away under Dax's hands and mouth. My God, the wonderful and wicked things that man did to me. He put his lips, tongue, and fingers in places I never dared imagine another would touch me. I fell to pieces and was put back together.

Not even Wren's hostility, which radiated from across the room, hindered what had happened. I simply pretended he wasn't there—until it was over and his hatred brought me back to reality.

Dax warned me the ride to Dyhurst—an ancient castle perched on the southern edge of Rygard—would be arduous. He hadn't exaggerated. We remain off the main road, traveling a barely trodden path through a forest that is nothing like Blithe. Here, it is lush and lovely. So very much alive. I do my best to miss nothing. Commit every nuance of Rygard to memory. Fill my mind with as many sights as possible to compensate for my lost years.

Dax maintains a steady conversation, speaking to me in hushed tones throughout the grueling morning. Quinn had ridden ahead of us for much of the time. The reason, Dax explained, is his sharper senses ensure we're traveling a safe path. And Wren, blessedly, hasn't spoken more than a handful of words to me, if even that much. Good. I have enough to worry about to make it through the arduous hours without the burden of his foul temper.

I shift and press my back against Dax's chest. "Dax?" Foolish me to think riding a horse would be simple. How difficult could it be? You just…sit. Wrong. The saddle is grueling, and I'm inching closer to tears with each step the horse takes.

"Aye, Little Captive?"

My cheeks flame at what I'm about to demand. "We need to stop for a moment."

"Wren won't like it."

"If we don't stop, we'll have to finish the journey sitting in a puddle. I'm sure that will make for a soggy situation."

That puts an abrupt end to any argument he might have voiced. "Wren, Quinn," Dax shouts. "Rapunzel needs a rest."

"No," Wren snaps.

I glance at Dax over my shoulder, imploring him with my eyes. "This is not a request."

Shrugging, he slows his steed to a stop.

I sag with relief. "Thank you."

"Don't thank me yet. You're the one who has to suffer Wren's temper."

I'd rather endure Wren's wrath than ride in piss-soaked clothing. I irritate the animal with my clumsy dismount. My muscles are stiff, and the moment my feet connect with the ground, needles shoot up my legs. Somehow, though, I sprint toward the thicket and add proper horsemanship to the growing list of things I must learn if I live long enough to see my way out of the mess the king has made of Rygard.

"Dax," Wren thunders. "Did I not say she's to go nowhere alone?"

Boots hit the ground. Heavy footsteps follow me. Desperation overrides mortification as I duck behind a wide tree, grab a handful of leaves, and hitch up my skirts. I let out an audible sigh as I empty my bladder, not even caring if Wren unleashes his fury on me right here and now.

"For fuck's sake, Wren, leave her alone," Dax shouts.

The footsteps stop. "You and your kind fucking heart."

Dax's laughter rings out across the glade. "Would I have those words in blood, because just days ago, I believe it was you who accused me of being a callous whoremonger."

"You do consort with whores," Quinn drawls.

"The only people I consort with are the two of you," Dax retorts with a laugh. Then louder for my benefit, "Until, of course, I met our fair Rapunzel."

After making use of my leaves and smoothing my skirts, I step from the trees—and nearly collide with Wren. "Time will prove to Dax what a selfish bitch you are."

I clasp my hands together to stop myself from slapping the insult from his mouth. "Let me pass, Wren."

"Such authority coming from a powerless girl." He steps closer, slicing away the space between us. "This is the part in the story where I make plain your role in it. You may be free of the tower, poor, pathetic Rapunzel, but you're still a prisoner." Quick as a lightning strike, his fist twines in my hair at the nape of my neck. His beautiful face fills everything I see. "Am I at all unclear?"

"No," I grit out to appease his need for domination.

"Good." His eyes cut so deeply into mine I swear he sees every depraved thought I've had of him. Even now, I can't hide the sinful things I want him to do to me. Things far more decadent than what his friends and I did this morning. When my gaze travels to his mouth, then down his chest to his groin, his sharp words snap my eyes right back to his face. "I'm not Dax or Quinn. I told you. You need to earn my cock, and unless you also have magic that reverses time, that will *never* happen."

Then I hear the whistle of wind through the trees. A sound so subtle that if Wren didn't tilt his head at the faint trill, I would have paid it no mind. But he releases me with a hard shove that sends me stumbling backward. Confused, I scan the landscape but see nothing. "Wren, what—"

"Quiet," he hisses.

Suddenly Quinn is behind me, sword out, and I realize the whistle was his way of warning Wren of trouble. Those disturbing black eyes scan the landscape as he grabs my arm and pulls me back into the tree line. He forces me to crouch in the brush. "Stay put and be silent."

I nod and crouch low, tucking my braid under me to make myself as small as possible. My heart beats hard and heavy as I peer through the bramble, tracking the men as they lead their horses into the thicket. They're measured. Calm. Quinn's massive broadsword gripped tight in his right hand is the only hint of danger. Otherwise, there is nothing to suggest they suspect a threat lurks out of sight.

Once the horses are secure, they stalk away from the animals. I assume they do this to draw an impending confrontation away from our only means of transportation. I glance to my left, and there, watching us on a low rise a fair distance away, are two riders. One has a notched arrow trained on Wren. The sun glints off the other's sword as his horse snorts and paws the ground.

"Give us your goods and the girl, and we'll let you walk away with your lives," the man with the sword shouts.

Wren pulls free his sword. "Three against two says we keep our goods and the girl."

"Or I can put this arrow through your heart," the one with the loaded longbow counters.

"You could," Wren drawls, his tone bored. "But you still won't make it out of this glade alive."

Quinn rotates the wrist of his sword arm, twirling the weapon. "Actually, it's four against three. There's more behind us." Two enormous men, armed with broadswords, reveal themselves from within the thicket. They stroll up behind us, and I sink lower. "And I still say we'll keep our goods *and* the girl."

Even from my poor vantage point, I see Quinn's midnight eyes spark with anticipation.

Dax rolls his neck over his shoulders, then casts the two men an eager grin. "Can we begin this bloodbath? I'd like to get it done so there's time to bathe before I fuck your women since

Twisted

you won't be making it home." He nods at the youngest of the men. "Or maybe… How old is your mother?"

Oh, Lord, did he…?

"This asshole said he's going to tup my mother." His yell reaches the men on the hill.

"No," Dax corrects him. "I implied I was going to fuck her. Raw, like an animal."

The kid snarls, and when he charges toward Dax, hell erupts around me.

An arrow flies by Wren, nearly striking his neck. I slap my hands over my mouth to stifle my cry, but my God, if anything happens to him… I'll rip every hair from my head to save him.

I've read a lifetime's worth of books. Some of my favorites depicted great battles. Those pages failed to capture the noise and chaos of an actual fight. They couldn't express the vibration of horses' hooves as they beat against the ground. The entire world seems to quake under the clash of steel as Dax and Quinn fend off their opponents.

But Wren, an archer at heart, sheaths his swords and grabs the longbow slung across his torso. He pulls an arrow from his quiver, notches it, aims, and strikes the mounted attacker charging toward him.

Takes him down with a single shot to the eye.

Sybil told me how John's father died in the same manner. The rumor, she said, is that Percy Kincaid fired the shot that killed King Henry. After today, I have to wonder if the tale is more fact than fiction because, with everything I know about Wren, one thing is paramount—his father trained him well.

Quinn's mounted adversary gets dangerously close to cleaving him in twain. I choke back a scream when the rider slices Quinn's left arm. Quinn, thank God, doesn't seem affected by it. He glances at the injury, and…laughs. While his opponent turns his horse for another go, Quinn raises his sword to point at the rider. "That scratch will cost your life."

Quinn effortlessly, and not hindered at all by his bleeding arm, thwarts the next attack in a movement so fast and fluid I would have missed it if I blinked. The rider, confused as his horse slows to a stop, blinks blankly at the spray of blood covering Quinn. Then he gapes in horror at what's left of his stump of a mutilated leg.

His wail pierces my ears like daggers, and I gag at that severed limb lying in the dirt. The man slides off his horse, and the animal runs off into the thicket. Quinn doesn't waste a moment. He strides over to the defeated man, and with his tattooed fingers curled tight around his sword's hilt, rolls his eyes with disgust.

"You should have heeded my friend's warning." Then he drives his blade deep into the man's chest, cutting bone as easily as if he were slicing through air.

The coppery tang of blood and sweat and fear and death... Putrid odors my books also failed to accurately convey. How could they? Or maybe they did, and it was me, having experienced nothing but my tower, who couldn't grasp the vivacity of their words? And as I watch Quinn rip the blade free from the man's chest, I know I'll never *un*see this. *Un*smell this. Then he focuses on me. Primal demonic thrill corrupts every feature on his face. I can't deny that he is a magnificent monster, and when he wipes the blood from his face with the back of his hand, I nod to assure him I'm unharmed. Then he joins Wren and Dax, both making quick work of the other assailants.

Wren has his attacker off his horse. Their swords cross again and again as they move together in a brutal dance. Wren is a breathtaking sight of barely constrained, brutal power. There is nothing left of the grubby boy who would sneak to the tower to visit me. He is ruthless. Wielding that weapon with the skill and grace of a man born to battle. Even when it seems the outlaw gains the upper hand, Wren counters the strike and makes quick work of impaling him through the right shoulder. He slides in deep, twisting. Grinding steel against bone until the man's weapon slips from his grip.

Heaving, Wren pulls free his blade. "Your stupidity and greed got you all killed."

"Go fuck yourself," the defeated man spits.

"Your arrogance is admirable but grossly unearned." A sinister grin curls Wren's lips a moment before he swipes his sword across the man's throat, opening a deep gash along his neck.

The outlaw drops to his knees. He gurgles out the most awful sounds as he drowns in his blood. Wren steps back when the man tips forward to land facedown at his feet. He jumps over his kill and darts toward Dax, but that battle is all but finished. Quinn has the beaten outlaw's arms pinned behind his back. Dax, the scoundrel, antagonizes the man by waving a dagger in front of his face.

"Now it's three against one. I should let my soulless friend here"—Dax taunts him, motioning to Quinn with the dagger—"have fun ripping you to shreds." Then he leans in close and snarls in the man's face, "Was it worth it?"

I have to shift positions for a better view, and when I do, I see how badly they battered the man. He's bleeding from…well, everywhere. I doubt he could stand if Quinn wasn't holding him.

"The king has taxed this province to the point of starvation," he rasps between cracked lips. "We have no choice but to loot travelers."

Dax holds the weapon so close to the outlaw's terrified eye that even I cringe. "Life, I've learned, is about choices. For instance, you made a mistake when you took things too far by demanding our woman."

The man chokes on a mouthful of blood. He spits it out before answering. "Can't blame a man for trying."

"Aye," Dax agrees, "I can, and I do, you fucking fool."

His audacity forces me out of my hiding spot. Quinn sees me

first. He rolls his eyes and lets out a growl that has Wren swinging around, sword still in hand to eye whatever threat is charging up behind them. He lowers his weapon when he realizes it's me, but his glare fries me as I approach.

"No one told you to come out yet," Wren grumbles.

Ignoring him, I shove an amused Dax aside and march up to the defeated outlaw. "You are despicable."

He stops squirming and blinks his one good eye at me. The other is swollen shut. His mouth drops open, and he works on words that seem stuck to the back of his throat. Behind me, Wren grunts out a curse, and when finally the man speaks, he utters, "You are a vision." His strained voice cracks. He adds, "Like an angel."

Thunderstruck by his odd remarks, I simply gape at him until Dax pulls me away and shoves me at Wren. He catches me, then releases me like I'm a plague. Wren wipes his hand on his breeches as if touching me is the vilest thing under the sun.

"Make this fucking quick." Wren barks the order at Dax. He drags a scowl over me. "We've been delayed long enough."

"You know I hate making my fucking quick." Dax scrapes the blade down the man's lacerated cheek. He releases a loud, frustrated sigh. "Well, you heard the man. You got lucky."

That's the only warning Dax affords him.

Quinn grabs the man's hair and yanks it upward, extending his neck. Dax steps back and raises his sword. He separates the head from the body in one rapid and brutal swing. It happens so swiftly, so cleanly, with the tip of the blade inches from slicing Quinn. The barbaric move proves the trust these men have for each other and how they can predict each other's movements.

And oh, God. Quinn tosses the severed head away like trash. Dax gives a dramatic shiver, with Wren complaining that the latter takes nothing seriously. But my focus falls back on the body, disgusted as I watch blood seep from the mutilated neck. It drops like a sack of broken bones, and I swear, I almost lose what little food I ate this morning.

Wren turns and scorches me with a scathing glare—as if I'm the origin of this carnage. I suppose I am in his mind because I'm the reason we stopped.

One more sin he can throw at me.

The men go to the horses to wash the blood from their hands and faces. Quinn bandages his wound on his outer biceps, and, quick as a flash, we're ready to leave.

Dax takes my hand and walks me toward his horse. "Wren can hold a mean grudge. I don't envy your task of trying to earn his forgiveness."

These men might know Wren, but I do as well. However, the person we know are vastly different people. I see the battle of those two selves reflected in his turbulent brown eyes. Each side of himself is striving for dominance. Each fighting to erase the other. One is the damaged and angry man he's become. The other is the boy who came to the tower year after year. In the rain, snow, heat, and cold. To keep a lonely little girl company. That person is still there, buried under layers of pain, and I haven't loved Wren for twelve years to give up on him now.

Grabbing my waist, Dax lifts me onto the saddle. Numbly, I swing my leg over the animal, with Dax climbing up behind me. I settle against his hard chest, taking comfort in his strength.

"He can't hate me forever."

"We'll see, Little Captive," is all he says.

Wren canters his horse past us, taking the lead. "No stopping until we reach the Soren River."

Quinn falls in behind him, throwing me a smirk. He is still speckled with blood. Between that and his scar, he looks every bit like a demon shot straight up from hell. But he doesn't scare me. He bleeds, which means he's still more man than monster. And although I have no life experience beyond the tower, I know this...

I've felt the grass beneath my feet.
The sunlight on my face.
I'm learning to ride a horse.
Two men pleasured me in two different ways.
And I saw four men die right before my eyes.

I can't go back to living as Sybil's willing captive. Not now, after tasting so much of the world in such a tiny amount of time.

Imagine what adventure awaits me tomorrow.

King John must die.

It's the only way I can truly live.

Chapter Fifteen

WREN

"What's it like being…magical?" Dax's question breaks the monotony of the overcast morning. He hesitates on the last word of the sentence. "Does it feel different?"

Rapunzel's reluctance to answer fills the air with a tangible tension. She watches the southern Rygard landscape as we ride by, staring off at the distant a. "Different from what? I know nothing else." Her slight shoulders lift and drop in a small shrug. "This is all I've ever been."

"So, how's it work?" Quinn voices the question that's haunted me since the day in The Cup and Crown when I learned Rapunzel possesses the power to heal.

What I hadn't realized is that Quinn is equally curious. But I should have expected he'd be…invested…especially given his rather enthusiastic response to her yesterday morning. Sweet hell. Yesterday morning. It took all my discipline not to pull Dax from between her legs and stuff her full of my cock. To finally sate the primal need to fuck her that's been burning inside me since I was sixteen. To leave my mark upon her flawless body, showing Rygard that I own its most sacred treasure.

Her movement is graceful when she touches her hair, her fingers trailing along the thick braid. Last night, we made camp by the bank of the Soren River, and while Dax assured Rapunzel we'd give her privacy, she politely declined to bathe. We three, however, took advantage of the refreshing water and washed off the afternoon's battle.

The injury to Quinn's arm, although still mending, isn't severe—for him. If either Dax or I had been on the receiving end of that blow, the outcome would have been devastating.

"I suppose it doesn't matter. Not anymore." She glares pointedly at me, those green eyes full of accusation.

"What doesn't *matter*, Rapunzel?" I demand.

"If I tell you the story." She pulls her gaze off me, gathers her heavy braid, and lays it across her lap. "My mother fell ill during her pregnancy. Desperate, my father called on a witch to save her, but it was too late. My mother was beyond even Sybil's power. But the spell had been cast, and the magic flowed from her failing body to mine. For the duration of the pregnancy, I was the only thing that kept her alive." Rapunzel drags in a trembling breath. Her sad stare sees past the barren landscape. As if she's viewing ghosts through someone else's eyes. "She died the moment I was born. And my father... Sybil said he changed in that instant. All that was good and kind in him died along with his wife. When he saw my hair, how it glowed golden, she glimpsed my future. To save me from him, Sybil claimed I died as well, and used a spell to prove her lie. They entombed me in my mother's arms. But Sybil came for me while I lay in a sleep-death state. She stole me from the crypt and brought me to the tower. That's where I stayed, mostly alone, for twenty-four years."

Dax wraps an arm around her and hugs her tight against his chest. "So, Wren had it wrong. Sybil was protecting you."

Rapunzel releases a long breath and swipes wispy hair away from her face. "Sybil was never the villain."

Twisted

"Thank fuck." Dax unwraps himself from her and kisses the back of her head. "I wasn't looking forward to killing a witch."

Rapunzel opens her mouth to say something to him, but Quinn silences her by snapping in his typical ruthless way, "Tragic tale. Now finish it."

"There's not much more to tell. Sybil never held me against my will. I voluntarily remained in the tower to protect Rygard." She bounces her gaze from Quinn to me. "Can you imagine the harm someone could inflict upon this kingdom if my hair fell into the wrong hands?"

"Your hair?" There's a note of amusement in Dax's tone. "No wonder it has a glow to it. Now it makes sense."

Rapunzel gives him an ardent nod. "Sybil never understood why the magic settled there, but it did. She uses small amounts to keep herself young and healthy so she can protect me."

I let out a vile curse hearing her finally say this aloud. It sends liquid rage through my veins and brings me back to the days when I sat at my father's bedside and watched his body rot from the poison the king fed him.

Goddamn you, John.

The king once told me his kingdom has its secrets. Secrets he might one day call on me to protect. I hadn't realized then that my father may have already known those secrets. Perhaps he got too close. Saw too much, and John murdered him for it.

Maybe my father discovered John's obsession with finding Rapunzel.

If he had control over her healing abilities, the king could render himself damn near immortal. He could use it to keep his soldiers fit on the battlefield. John could rule Rygard—and beyond—indefinitely.

"Wren." Rapunzel's voice pulls me out of my thoughts, but I don't look at her. I can't. "Your father... I'm sorry. If I had saved him—"

"Don't you dare say it, Rapunzel." Jaw locked, I grind my

molars against a surge of fury. "One more goddamn word about him, and I swear on all that's holy, I'll cut out your fucking tongue."

We fall silent and stay that way for a long while, trotting into Harlow, the southernmost region in Rygard. Another hour and we'll arrive at Dyhurst. Finally. Feels like we haven't been home in ages.

But leave it to Dax to ruin a perfectly good quiet by posing a question to Rapunzel. "What happened to your father?"

She slides me a cautious look before answering. "Sybil told me he eventually died of a broken heart." Rapunzel's soft but emotionless reply catches on the summer breeze. "He couldn't live without his wife, nor with the knowledge his daughter killed her."

"The fuck. He blamed you?" Quinn snarls.

Rapunzel bows her head. "I'm blamed for many things beyond my control."

Her barb strikes true, but it's not the same. She chose to stay in her precious tower. Then she decided against saving my father. Rapunzel didn't murder her mother. Her father was obviously a sick bastard. If he wasn't already dead, I'd find him and kill him myself.

"What do you believe?"

Rapunzel's silence at Quinn's question speaks volumes.

I hope that piece of shit is rotting in hell...

...even as I tell myself I don't care about Rapunzel.

Not at all.

"I'd offer my condolences, but you don't sound broken up over the loss," Dax remarks, breaking the tension.

She lets out a sad little sigh. "I never knew the man, and I don't think I would like him if I did."

"Where was this witch when Wren was visiting you for years?" Quinn demands.

"Secrets are funny things. They thrive no matter how hard

Twisted

one works to keep them contained." She lifts her head, and although she answers Quinn, she turns to the left and nails me with those wistful green eyes. "To thwart anyone who might know I exist, Sybil travels relentlessly across Rygard, spreading false information about my location."

"Smart." Quinn sounds impressed by Sybil's tactic.

"Must have been lonely in that tower," Dax adds.

"It was, for many years." A tear slips down Rapunzel's cheek. She wipes it away and stares off at the mountains. "Until it wasn't."

Chapter Sixteen

QUINN

The best thing about Dyhurst Castle is that its roof and walls are intact. Also, it sits on a cliff that overlooks the Lennox Sea.

The violent waves rip across the surface, crashing against the crag as I stand on the parapet peering through the cracked crenellations. I stare into the horizon and watch the dawn, wondering how the hell we got to this place. How one man's madness has destroyed countless lives. On mornings such as these, while the castle is still quiet, it's like glimpsing the awakening of heaven. This fleeting moment—this perfect stillness—the burden of my curse lifts, and I am free…

But once the sun crests, it sheds light on the countryside and shatters the illusion. The familiar weight drags me back into the darkness. It blots out the sunlight. Suffocates me. Fury turns my blood to poison as it slides through my veins.

It leaves me helpless to fight against the cold and the fear that tightens around my throat. Choking me. Inching me closer to the day when death will take me, and the demon who owns me will claim what's rightfully his.

Until then, these quietest moments are the loudest—because I did everything within my power to save my sister.

And I still failed her.

I couldn't save her when my father and her betrothed bargained her away to a monster.

It's in the silence when I hear the echo of her screams the loudest.

Some days, when the shame and regret consume me, I wish Wren would have let me die. It would have been a more merciful fate. But then I remember what awaits me, and each breath I take is worth the effort to stay alive.

"Quinn?"

I whip around at the sound of my name on Rapunzel's tongue. Her hair is wild around her lithe body, falling to her knees in golden waves. She's a single drop of purity in my sea of sin, wearing only a white chemise. The material billows around her in the summer breeze. Her flesh still carries the faint scent of the rose soap she used in her bath last night after we arrived at Dyhurst. And with her watching me under the dawn's glow, she's a vision pulled from my darkest fantasy.

"What do you want, Rapunzel?" Fuck me, but I didn't mean for that to come out so harshly.

"It's lovely up here." She walks toward the edge of the crenelated parapet, her captivating green eyes filled with wonder as she gazes at the horizon. She places her hands on a chipped merlon, a dazzling smile lifting her lips. "And peaceful."

"It was." There it is again, my automatic scathing response, but in my defense, she asked for it by coming here and disturbing my moment of tranquility.

Her expression drops when she absorbs the meaning of my words. She wraps her arms around her torso and walks backward as if to ward off my hostility. "I apologize for bothering you."

But does she have to look like I spit in her face?

I close my eyes and pinch the bridge of my nose. "You're

not," I grind out between clenched teeth. "Just..." I reopen my eyes and lower my hand, releasing a loud sigh. "Don't you have something better to do than walk the battlements?"

"I wouldn't know." She tentatively takes in the splendor of the surrounding landscape. "I wasn't exactly given a tour when we arrived. I'm a prisoner, remember? Maybe if someone explained my purpose in Wren's plan, I would have a task to occupy me. I tried to question him after he dumped me in a bedchamber last night. Would you like to hear what he told me? He said I ask too many questions and slammed the door in my face."

That certainly sounds like Wren.

From what he told us about Rapunzel, I expected a docile, selfish pawn in his revenge against John. Rapunzel might be soft-spoken, cautious even, but she's far from timid. It's fair to say that after what she allowed Dax and I to do with her at the inn, she's caged fire, and if Wren doesn't play this right, we'll be the ones who get burned.

Especially seeing her now, scowling at me for all she's worth. Not in the least intimidated when other women are smart enough to run from me.

Or maybe it's because she spent her life trapped in a tower, and she's too ignorant to know when danger is staring her in the face.

"You think Wren owes you an explanation?"

She drops her arms and fists her hands at her side. "I do, yes."

The audacity.

"He doesn't owe you a damn thing."

We stay locked in a silent battle, eyeballing each other for a damn long while as the sun climbs higher. Then she turns away to watch the waves batter the cliff. The woman is a glimpse of paradise in this bleakest corner of Rygard. And fuck me if I don't want to reach out and—

"Quinn, may I ask you a question?"

And this is why I curse my moment of weakness at the inn. Give a little, and next thing you know, you're giving too much. "Will you ask me regardless of my answer?"

"Yes, I suppose I will." With my shirt open and the demon's marks on full display, she studies the black vine-like tattoos that wind their way around and up my torso. They snake around my hands, arms, and neck, stopping under my chin. "Are you a man?"

No matter how hard I try, I can't hold back my strangled laugh at her bold question. "Do you want to know if I have a cock, Rapunzel?"

Color blooms in her cheeks. "No, I'm asking why your eyes are black and your body bears those demonic marks."

I heave out a sigh and run a hand through my hair. I contemplate withholding the truth but decide against it. There's no point in lying. Besides, Rapunzel was honest with us, and she deserves like measure.

"I surrendered my soul to a demon," I admit without hesitation or emotion.

Rapunzel, however, doesn't accept my answer with the same detachment. Appalled, her eyes go wide, and she slaps a hand over her mouth. She even backs away. And when she finally drops her hand to her heart, she asks, "Why would you do such a thing?"

I shrug with feigned indifference because I don't want her fucking pity. "It seemed the smart thing to do at the time."

She rakes her gaze over me. Takes a step closer. Then backs away again. Slams her brows into a frown. All the while, her every emotion and question play out across her face. "Are you going to steal my soul?"

"Tempting, but no." I kick my lips up in a smirk. "It's not your soul I'm after."

Then her jaw works on empty words before finding her voice

again. "What could have possibly happened that would cause you to barter away your soul?" Courageously, she steps toward me and presses her warm hand against my chest. It takes all I have to keep my breath even and my heartbeat steady. "Dear God, Quinn."

"God can't help me." There's resignation and acceptance in my voice. With her this close, I notice the most minute details of her. The subtle things mortal eyes don't see. Like the golden metallic flecks almost hidden in the lush green of her eyes. Each frantic beat of her heart echoes in my head. Her rushing blood is louder than a rapid river's roar. I need to consume her until I don't know where she ends, and I begin. "I'm no longer in His good graces."

"The demon gave you strength. I saw as much when you fought those men." Rapunzel glides her fingers over the black designs that decorate my chest without a hint of concern for her safety. Her touch leaves a fire trail in its wake, melting the ice that's lived inside me since the day I summoned the demon and offered it the one thing I possessed that had value. "Did you receive other evils in exchange for your soul?"

"Evils?" An apt word if ever there was one.

She shifts her attention to my eyes, and that's when I reluctantly sense it—a kinship with this woman I don't want or fucking need. "Sybil calls my ability to heal a gift, but she's wrong. I could freely share it with the world if it were a gift. Instead, I have to hide lest someone use it nefariously." She lowers her gaze, shame radiating from her in waves. "So, yes, Quinn, evils, because people like us, the power we possess... It is no gift."

Rapunzel is wrong, but I don't correct her misconception. What lives inside her is a blessing. What dwells in me is something ugly.

Something rotten.

But it has its advantages...

"My vision and hearing are sharper. An injury that would kill an average man is a mere scratch to me." Although I initially had no intention of sharing so much of myself with anyone other than Wren and Dax, the words spill out naturally from my mouth, almost like a confession. "And I have the power to rip the life out of you with the ease of pulling the wings off a fly."

I leave unsaid how it takes all of my energy to do it, which is why I've done it once.

One time.

That moment haunts me every moment of every fucking day.

No son should kill his father—and never the way I murdered mine.

"Will you tell me why you sacrificed your soul?"

The answer is there, stuck at the back of my throat, begging to be set free. What would it matter if Rapunzel knew? But when I open my mouth, I can't speak of that day. The memory is a blade that cuts through my hollowed chest. It hacks me to pieces. Bleeds me. Leaves me deader inside than the demon did the night it reached into me, tore out my soul, and left me cold and shivering like rancid meat.

"No," is all I say, and it's enough because Rapunzel nods her understanding and offers me a comforting smile that doesn't do a damn thing to quiet the rage that simmers inside me.

"I don't ever want to return to the tower now that I've seen the beauty of the world beyond its walls." She continues to track the marks on my body, her gentle touch driving me mad. "Does that make me a selfish person?"

Fuck, but this Sybil scrambled Rapunzel's mind. Warped it to where Rapunzel believes she owes this entire kingdom her freedom.

"You're never going back." Unable to resist, I thread my fingers through the silken mass of her hair. Fist it in my scarred hand, the strands snagging on the calluses that ruin my palms.

Whether it's the wind or emotion that cause tears to well in her eyes, I neither know nor care. "I never asked for any of this, Quinn."

I tug her head back, my gaze fixed on her plush lips. "That's the way of war, Rapunzel. We rarely choose the battle, only how bloody we're willing to get to win."

Rapunzel's lips part, and her cheeks flush. Her small breasts rise and fall with each rapid breath. I smell her desire, and it stokes something primal inside me. Has me do something foolish. Something I'm sure I'll regret.

Especially when I succumb to the feral need to taste her.

I graze my mouth over hers hoping it will scratch the itch. All it does is awaken an even deeper and darker craving. Rapunzel snakes one arm around my waist and presses herself against me. I part her lips with my tongue and dive inside. She's so small. Delicate. It's like trying to hold the petal of a flower without tearing it.

Too bad with me, she doesn't get gentle. For that, there's Dax. With me, she gets a ruined creature who will offer her pain with her pleasure.

Rapunzel, however, is giving as good as I give her.

Her hands are all over me. Meets each sweep of my tongue and every rock of my hips. I swallow her desperate moan and answer with a growl as I grip her leg and hike it high, pinning it to my side as I grind my raging cock against her core.

I break away to allow her to drag in a breath. "Why don't you care that Wren gave us leave to use you?"

Her lips, swollen from my kiss, lift in a mischievous grin that shoots straight to the tip of my aching dick. "I've spent a lifetime numb, believing I would die alone. Untouched and unloved. So, who said I'm not also using you?"

Appalled, I drop her leg. "You'll find no love here, Rapunzel."

Best she accepts this cruel truth now. For her sake and ours.

I'll not have a simpering girl chasing us around, seeking the impossible and making herself a nuisance.

"Love, I've learned, is a sentiment found only in books. It will never be my reality." She draws her hands down my neck, to my chest. Lower still, her fingers linger on the waistband of my breeches, scorching my already heated flesh. "What I want is to experience life."

Bold words.

Let's test the courage of Rapunzel's convictions.

"Get on your knees."

Rapunzel hesitates, but just for a moment. Then she drops, hitting the ground, her face level with my groin. I have to suck in a long, steadying breath to keep from tugging down my breeches and fucking her face until she weeps. I'm not a goddamn animal, despite how badly I crave this woman—and have since Wren told us about her.

Even before I saw her, I needed her.

Wren may claim she's a coward, but I know the truth now. Rapunzel's soul is pure. Unsoiled by the ugly of this world. If Wren weren't blinded by grief and rage, he'd see she's nothing like John and innocent of his sins.

But it's not my place to set him right. This is something he needs to work out for himself.

And after years of carrying the weight of my guilt, I need that burden lifted—even for a stolen moment on this rotting parapet by a girl with magic hair.

Rapunzel stares up at me, her huge eyes bright and expectant. "What do I do?"

"You claimed you are using us." I unlace my breeches. Part the brown leather and free my throbbing cock. "Prove it."

Her gaze bounces from my face to my cock. The heat of her stare sends a rush of blood to my shaft. My balls tighten as she slides her hands up my thighs. When her tentative fingers curl around the waistband of my pants, I forget how to breathe. She draws my breeches over my hips and down my legs until they stop at my calves, catching on the tops of my black leather boots. I release the air trapped in my lungs, and watch, fascinated, as she licks her lips.

That damn tongue.

I need it on me as much as I need my next breath.

Her eyes have a curious glint. "I don't know how to do this."

Of course she doesn't, and her inexperience stokes my lust.

"Open your mouth." I issue the gruff command between clenched teeth, barely holding myself together.

She complies quickly, easily, and without a hint of reluctance caused by ridiculous societal shames. With my other hand, I grab the base of my dick and guide the tip to her lips. She closes her eyes, her fingers biting into my thighs as I slide into her mouth. She drowns out my hiss with her moan. The sound vibrates against my shaft. Keeping a tight hold on her hair, I rock forward, rubbing along her flattened tongue until I hit the back of her throat. Her whimper is such a saccharine sound, mingling with the crash of the waves that batter the cliff below us. I pull out and run myself across her bottom lip. Then sink back inside her mouth, relishing the wet warmth that welcomes me.

But Rapunzel doesn't kneel idly between my legs.

She's clumsy at first, all awkward teeth and disjointed bobbing. But once she finds her rhythm, I silently acknowledge that I'll take one moment in her mouth rather than eternity in heaven.

"Fuck." She swirls her tongue around my tip. Sucks me deep. I loosen my grip on her hair, now just holding the heavy mass out of her way as she explores every part of my cock. I enjoy the unobstructed view of her swallowing me, and fuck if it isn't...everything.

Her hands trail along my hips, finding their way around to my ass. Her fingers dig into me as she pumps her head over my swollen length. Every eager pull sends another wave of heat crashing through me as she brazenly learns how to pleasure a man.

Learns how to pleasure *me*.

Every hiss and groan I make encourages her to suck harder. When her teeth accidentally graze me, she shifts and tries something new. Rapunzel is more than a quick learner—she's also devious. This woman changes tactics. She moves off my cock to tease me. To lick her way up to the tip with light kisses until I want to toss her on the ground, rip off her chemise, and fuck her until the stone beneath us cracks from the force of my thrusts.

"I wonder." She cups my taut balls. "Are these as sensitive as the rest of you?" With a guttural groan, I realign myself with her lips and thrust deep into her mouth.

And she takes it.

Rapunzel kneels there and takes everything I demand of her.

She's not coy. Not calculated. There is an honest curiosity as she experiments with different ways to torture me. When the painful pleasure builds at the base of my spine, working its way to my balls, I grab her hair and hold her head steady. She also takes that, opening her eyes to stare up at me as I spill down her throat, gagging her.

Only once I empty every last drop do I release her hair and step backward, putting space between us. Allow her to spit out the excess and wipe her mouth. Rapunzel draws in the salty sea air, then directs those dazed eyes at me, and I swear on all that's holy, she can see straight to my blackened heart. I tuck myself in my breeches, then I beckon her to me with a crook of my finger.

Rapunzel stands and has the audacity to shake her head. I lift a brow and extend my hand. Again, she denies me.

I drop my arm. "You deliberately try my patience?"

The infuriating woman takes her time in closing the distance between us. She has a way about her. Rapunzel is graceful. Each step fluid. Her hips sway with her hair floating around her like a golden cloud. It's easy to see why the king would destroy his kingdom to gain her—magical hair or not.

Once Rapunzel is in range, I grab her. Spin us around and slam her against the ragged castle wall.

"What are you doing?"

I trace a finger along her plump bottom lip. "Anything I want."

I kiss her throat just to sample the flavor of her flesh. That's what I tell myself. But everything about this woman demands I take more. That I take all of her. But I hold back because although Wren said we could use Rapunzel however we want, Dax and I agreed to leave one part of her intact. To leave one part of her for him—even if it kills us not to take what she so exquisitely offers.

And my God, does she offer…

Rapunzel arches her back and buries her hands in my hair when I yank down the neckline of her chemise and suck the peak of her bare breast in my mouth. I've never heard another woman whisper my name as reverently as she does. It sends a chill racing up my spine. I kick her legs apart. Hitch up her skirt. Seek her warmth because I need to be inside her, even if it's only with my fingers.

I stretch her, and Rapunzel grips my shoulders, crying out a lyrical mix of pleasure and pain. Panting, she rocks her hips in time with each thrust of my fingers up into her. She begs me for more. To go deeper. Harder. And I do. Giving her what she needs…

Until I don't.

Because it's more fun to tease, same as the devious woman did with me.

I withdraw my fingers and taunt her clit. Circle it and pinch it. Give her cunt a slap to shock the nerves. Torment her until Rapunzel squeezes her eyes closed. Covers my hand with hers and whimpers with frustration.

"Look at me, Rapunzel."

She obeys, opening her eyes. "It...hurts."

"Good." I can't wait for her body to strangle my cock when I'm inside her. "Remove your hand and keep your eyes on me."

She obeys without hesitancy and grips my shoulders as I continue to torture her clit. Her lovely little cries are the sweetest music. When I slide my fingers slowly, so fucking slowly, inside her, she hisses in a long, hard breath. Her desire slicks my entry as I sink into her to the last knuckles.

"Just like that, Quinn. Please don't stop." She drips down my hand as I work her.

"When I fuck you, I'm taking your pussy and then I'm claiming your ass. You want that, don't you?"

She nods, panting and grinding against the thrusts of my fingers. "Yes. Oh, God, yes."

"And you'll beg me to fuck you harder." I push in deeper. "Until it hurts so good, you'll feel the stretch from my cock for days after I'm done with you."

"Quinn..." she breathes. Stray strands of gold whisper across her face in time with her heavy breathing.

"Now be my good girl and come for me." I crook my fingers inside her to rub along her walls.

Then, because I'm an evil motherfucker, I bite the side of her throat. *Hard.*

Her knees buckle, but I keep working her until her pussy stops pulsating. Only then do I withdraw from her and lick her cum from my fingers.

Smirking, I fix her chemise, covering her. "Now we're finished."

Her laughter at my arrogant remark stays with me long after I leave her standing on the parapet—as does the vision of her gazing out at the sea. Wren was right. Rapunzel truly is a work of art. Devastatingly beautiful and begging to be broken.

For the first time in two years, I can almost remember what it's like to have a soul.
Almost.
This time, though, it has a name.
Rapunzel.

Chapter Seventeen

RAPUNZEL

"It's nice to have another woman here." Emma shakes out a linen sheet before hanging it over a rope to dry under the sun.

I wipe sweat from my brow, the heat oppressive this afternoon. My arms and back ache, and it feels marvelous. It's good to be putting in a hard day's labor. This is living. Being out in the fresh air, with the lazy summer breeze thick with the aromas of the herbs that grow in the nearby garden. The clash of swords echo from the lists. Everyone busy with a task instead of wasting hours waiting.

Because that's what I did in the tower.

I waited.

Waited for morning to become afternoon. For afternoon to age to evening. Night to become morning. For Sybil to return with stories of her travels.

And I waited on Wren's visits.

Oh, God, how I waited, staring out my window, peering through the trees for signs of movement. For even the slightest sign of Wren.

But most of all, I waited to die. I waited as time passed

slowly over me, moment by moment, bringing me closer to the grave. I existed for existence's sake. The days filled with so much monotony and loneliness, death seemed the logical answer to end the constant misery.

But not here. Here, glorious, beautiful life thrives.

At first glance, Dyhurst is a decaying shell of a forgotten castle. That initial impression is shockingly deceptive. Once inside the formidable curtain wall, the ward is teeming with activity. Well, maybe that's a bit of an exaggeration. But it's not as dead as it appears from the outside. There is a garden with narrow paths between the beds surrounded by wattle fencing. Four goats and three plump pigs are penned near where Quinn and Dax spar on the lists. Both men present a fascinating—and terrifying—sight as they mock-battle shirtless under the brutal midday sun.

Vastly different in temperament, build, and fighting style, they are a dichotomy in movement and skill, with Quinn holding back against his friend. Muscles flex beneath his decorated flesh. I still feel those vine-like tattoos warm under my touch, and when he glances at me, his midnight eyes hold me captive as the memory of what we did yesterday morning sends a fresh rush of desire to the juncture of my thighs.

When I took Quinn in my mouth, I understood what it means to have someone at my mercy. His body was mine to pleasure, and for those precious moments, a man as powerful as him was mine to control.

It was nothing short of incredible.

The two men move with mesmerizing grace over the lists, locked in a deadly dance that, if this were an actual battle, Quinn could easily overtake Dax. Not that Dax isn't a fierce warrior in his own right. He's just no match for Quinn's dark strength. It's a testament to Quinn's ability to control his power.

When one attacks, the other defends. Then it's a subtle shift, wherein one or two expert swings puts the other person on the

Twisted

defensive. It is riveting and alarming and beautiful to witness such violent skill exerted with ease by two feral men who used those same hands to bring my body to unbridled pleasure.

With great effort, I drag my gaze from the men and do my best to engage with Emma. She's a lovely woman, not much older than me. The moment I stepped into the courtyard yesterday, she rushed over, took my hands in hers, and declared that we would be the very best of friends. She and I, Emma explained, are the only women here, and she hasn't left my side. I even got a grand tour of Dyhurst, during which she introduced me to the men who inhabit this castle…

…all of whom are renegades of the crown in one form or another.

Then she convinced Wren to let me participate in the upkeep of the castle. For that alone, Emma earned my eternal gratitude —and friendship.

Although the ancient keep remains intact, unfortunately, the decayed chapel is a sad shadow of its former glory—and presided over by a defrocked priest. It seems the church frowns upon rebellious clergy who openly dare to question religious doctrine that favors men and harms women.

Bless him.

Emma ushered me out of the decomposing building, whispering, "Poor Kenric is determined to save our souls."

He even believes there's hope for Quinn.

Emma tosses her thick chestnut braid over her shoulder. She has an enchanting spark of vivacity in her brown eyes. "Listen to me, going on about nonsense." She's been filling me in on local gossip while we tend to the laundry. As if I mind. Then she grabs another linen from her basket and shakes it out. "It's just nice to have a woman to talk with. These ornery pricks are only interested in eating, fighting, and fucking. Usually in that order."

I sputter out a laugh. "Well, you'll get no complaints from

me." I pull out a shirt, smooth it, and drape it over the rope. "I've waited a lifetime to gossip."

And have a female friend.

Emma lifts a brow as she hangs breeches on the rope. "Aye, I heard. Wren gave us an earful about you yesterday." She snatches the last shirt from the basket and tosses it on the rope. Then she comes around the wet clothing and plants her hands on her hips. Although she's a slender woman, her particular feminine strength and determination make her seem larger than life. "He told us you're the reason our bastard king is destroying Rygard."

"Did he?" I stiffen and, instinctively, smooth my braid. "What else did he say?"

Emma motions to my head. "Also said you have magic hair." How blatantly spoken, the secret I spent my life captive to protect. But if Wren trusts these people, then I suppose I do as well. "Is it true?"

"Yes." I brace for rejection. Horror. Disgust. Covetousness. All the reactions Sybil warned me people would have if they knew the truth.

Emma takes my measure as if inspecting each golden strand of my hair. "Like how? Do you wrap it around the person? Sing a song?" She steps toward me, and I back away, but she keeps coming until she runs her hand over my braid. "How does the magic work?"

Well.

This isn't what I expected, and I almost weep with relief at Emma's questions.

"Sing a song? Good Lord, no." I finger a stray short brown lock that sprang loose from the plait. "I cut a small section, and when mixed with yarrow, comfrey, and woad, the hair dissolves into an elixir."

Emma pulls a face and steps back. "That's it? The person drinks it and it heals them?"

"Almost instantly." I remember the day Sybil returned to the tower with a broken arm after a rather nasty fall. It took moments for the bones to knit.

She tilts her head, blue eyes narrowing on the bits where Sybil clipped it to take tiny amounts to maintain her youth. This information I keep to myself. "I understand now why John wants you. He could make himself and his army practically invincible if he got his vile hands on you."

"That's why I stayed in the tower." I glance out over the courtyard, glad to be free but scared of all the things that could go wrong. I wonder if I was safer there, but John having destroyed Leeds, he had gotten too close. Dangerously close.

"That man is a monster. He slaughtered my family. He'll stop at nothing to find you." She shakes her head, and the sorrow in her eyes makes my heart ache for her. "He has no right to you. Whatever magic you have, Rapunzel, is yours, and he's not entitled to it." She comes at me and takes my hands. "John accused my father of treason. There was no proof, of course. None was needed. Nor was there a trial. Just the royal accusation and the remorseless slaughter of my family. That was his way of showing the consequences of questioning the king. I survived the attack only because the soldier who stabbed me was sloppy with his blade. Wren found me days later. I was hiding in a forest, near dead, and mad with grief. He brought me to Dyhurst, where he gave me a home and a family. But the true gift? Wren promised me revenge against John and retribution for Rygard."

I glance away and blink back the tears as her anguish flows into me. If hers were a physical pain, I would heal it to give her peace, but this… Heartache is something even I can't cure.

"I'm not sure what having a family means."

Emma embraces me, and it feels so natural. "You'll find it here, Rapunzel."

"That's my hope." But I doubt it if Wren gets his way.

Emma sets me at arm's length. "Although, I will warn you

that living with eleven men may have you thinking differently. They drive me mad sometimes if you want to know the truth. It's like living in a household of protective older brothers."

I laugh loud enough to gain Quinn and Dax's attention. They stop their training to watch us grab our empty laundry baskets and stroll toward the keep. We talk about our lives. Of the limited activities to keep the boredom at bay. And how she was the pampered middle daughter of Lord Gerold of Weston. But our pasts are painful, so we switch topics, with her explaining how she was at first scandalized living among these men, but then they swiftly became her family.

A glimpse around the courtyard—at the mismatched assortment of John's defectors—and I see Wren's beautiful collection of outcasts. All who now have a purpose other than only anger and revenge. They have a home and clan. It's everything I want right in front of me—if I dare defy Wren and make Dyhurst my home.

From the aroma of roasting meat wafting from the kitchen, I assume someone is preparing the evening meal. I want to lend a hand in there given that I gained a talent for cooking. Sybil rarely went near a pot or pan when she was at the tower. I will not be a burden to these people. I will work alongside them to keep this castle alive. And when Wren strolls into Dyhurst carrying two fat pheasants, my gaze is drawn to him before my mind catches up with the action. He may not be as wide as Quinn or as tall as Dax, but he filled out well since his days of visiting me in Blithe. But what I find truly vexing is that whenever I look at him, I find something new to appreciate —damn him.

I want to find him repulsive.

I need to hate him as he hates me.

Instead, a delicious rush settles at the juncture of my thighs at the thought of his hands on my body.

"That one is both saint and sinner." Emma catches me

Twisted

watching him and nudges me with her elbow. "He's got the devil's tongue but an angel's heart."

Truer words...

"I wish he'd direct his scowl elsewhere," I mutter.

She shakes her head as we round the corner of the keep, out of Wren's line of sight. "Scowl? Oh, Rapunzel, I wish a man would look at me the way Wren does you."

I've no idea what Emma sees. "Wren hates me."

"That's what you believe?" Why does Emma sound amused?

"That's what I know."

"Rapunzel, you have much to learn about the nature of people," she drawls.

I skid to a stop inside the hall, with Emma grabbing the basket from me and continuing ahead as I contemplate her remark. Faded tapestries of landscapes decorate the walls. The cozy sitting area doesn't seem as if it gets much use. The massive table, set in the center of the room, is as ancient and battled as the castle, and I wonder how many meals and conversations took place around it before this holding went to ruin.

Emma glances at me over her shoulder, a smile stretched across her pretty mouth and a mischievous sparkle in her eyes. I'm about to catch up to her, but Wren startles me by striding close beside me.

"She's right."

I frown at his gruff remark. "Pardon?"

"You have much to learn."

I toss up my hands and release a loud sigh. "Obviously. I spent the whole of my life moldering in a tower."

Wren, still holding those bloody pheasants, is stunningly untamed—and terribly Intimidating. I miss him, the Wren I fell in love with years ago. Because now, he feels a world away from me. My *inaction* contributed to the destruction of the beautiful carefree boy I fell in love with and replaced him with this cold and callous man.

"Emma said you intend to kill John. Is this true?"

His dark eyes, sizzling with anticipation of spilling royal blood, slice into me, and, for a moment, I fear he'll walk away. Leave me guessing. But he shocks me by growling, "Yes."

Oh.

Well.

"I see." I wring my hands as a riot of possibilities and fears run wild through my mind.

"Do you?" He snarls in my face. "And what do you think you see, Rapunzel?"

"A determined man with a dangerous obsession. Tell me, Wren, how do I factor in this plan?"

Wren lets out a nasty laugh and moves away, allowing me the space I need to breathe without inhaling the intoxicating scent of him. Still, he seems to take up all the space in the cavernous hall. The heat emanating from him does more to chase out the damp of the stone walls than the fire that blazes in the massive hearth across the chamber.

"It's simple, Rapunzel." Wren kicks up a brow and flicks his gaze over me as if I'm nothing more than an afterthought. "John wants you. As long as I have you, I hold all the power."

"So, I am your pawn?"

"You thought you had more value?"

Don't you dare cry.

I whip that around in my mind even as tears sting my eyes. "And when this war with the king is finished? What happens to me after, or did you not think that far ahead?"

"Oh, I thought ahead." Disgust laces his words. "Trust me, I thought long and hard and decided that after I murder John, I'm going to cut your fucking hair and make you watch while I burn every goddamn strand."

Those tears spill from my eyes to river down my cheeks. "I hope you do, and once the deed is done, I pray you find peace."

Unable to abide him one moment longer, I march from the

hall, half expecting him to stop me for no other reason than to yell at me for turning my back on him.

He doesn't, though, thank God.

I have no destination in mind, with most of the castle still a mystery. All I know is I need to flee the hall. Put as much distance as possible between Wren and me because I just learned a cruel lesson.

It's possible to love someone with your whole heart…

…and also hate them with your whole soul.

Chapter Eighteen

WREN

"John destroyed another village."

I pinch the bridge of my nose, my blood suddenly thick as sludge in my veins. It's been quiet for a full fortnight, with no reports coming to us of new attacks. Should have expected the reprieve would be short-lived. My hand instinctively moves to my sword, compelled by the need to run the weapon through the king's heart. "Which one?"

Quinn drops onto the chair opposite me in the hall's sitting area. The stressed wood groans under the sudden weight. He's dusty from the road and stinks of sweat and horse. "Haversville." He scratches a hand through his long, brown hair. A muscle tics in his jaw, his frustration palpable. "There were only a handful of survivors. Mostly women and children. They are...worse for the wear."

Of course they are, but even as I acknowledge this truth, I'm sickened damn near to death over what they must have suffered.

There is no honor among John's soldiers.

Haversville is dangerously close to Dyhurst—only a few hours' ride north. A slight push would bring John's soldiers to our doorstep. The only thing in our favor is that for all intents

Twisted

and purposes, the castle is believed to be abandoned. A forgotten relic perched on a barren cliff. The smart move is to remain here rather than risk Rapunzel out in the open while we seek another sanctuary. Still...

"Do we know the direction his army is heading?"

Anywhere but south.

"North." Quinn doesn't take his black eyes from the dancing flames that keep the chill of the stone walls at bay. "Our spies say the army split. Half are marching toward Trent. The others are picking their way toward Eastbury territory."

I release a relieved sigh and lean back in the chair. But where one problem is temporarily solved, the problem of Haversville remains. For the use of Dyhurst, we protect the surrounding area and keep Sir William Saunders well paid. Of course, it helps that William also loathes John and would welcome a Rygard free of the king's tyranny.

I curl my fingers around the weathered wood of the chair's arms, my gut coiled. More lives were lost. And for what? For John to make himself, and possibly his army, as close to immortal as humanly possible with Rapunzel's fucking hair. With that kind of power at his disposal, he could remake the world in his image. Set himself up as a god among men, with Rapunzel at his side, using her hair to keep himself young and healthy as Sybil has done throughout the years. It's enough to make me march out to the courtyard where she's helping Arthur in the garden and hack off every strand from her pretty head.

But at what cost?

Even now, much of her remains a mystery—but it's one I'm determined to solve.

"The last raid we pulled, when we intercepted those soldiers delivering that gold to John," I say to Quinn. "Give it to Warrick and tell him to distribute it to the survivors of Haversville. We can't leave those people to rot. That's not who we are." I lean forward as memories from the day the king ordered Leeds's destruction ambush me, flooding my mind with visions best left in the past. "If need be, he can gather supplies and volunteers from our allies in Leighton Falls."

"Of course." Quinn finally tears his gaze from the fire, and in those abysmal depths is a world of rage. He rests his arms across his thighs. "I would go myself, but with *her* here..."

I shake my head and lean back. "It's best if we stay." Then I see the question in his eyes. "What's on your mind, Quinn?"

"Our enchanted guest..." Quinn points to the ceiling. "What's to become of her?"

"Why do you care?"

"Answer the fucking question, Wren."

I don't particularly appreciate how Quinn is suddenly interested in my intentions for Rapunzel. Mainly because when I took her from the tower, I was covered in my mother's blood and filthy from her freshly dug grave. Even now, I want her to hurt as I hurt. I want to ruin her. Tear her apart. Put her back together wrong. Then leave her empty and aching—same as I am now.

Beyond that...

"I don't know," I admit.

Quinn purses his lips and returns to watching the flames flicker in the hearth. "Rapunzel is not the monster you need her to be."

"And you know this after a sennight spent listening to her lies."

Quinn slowly turns his head and levels me with a glare. "I'm well acquainted with evil, Wren, and that woman is—"

"My parents' blood is on her hands." Rapunzel may not be evil, but she's not innocent either.

"Wren—"

"If it was your father who John poisoned, and she denied you the means that would have saved his life, you would feel as I do," I reason, and then I visibly cringe when I realize my error.

"Actually," Quinn drawls, "I would offer her my undying gratitude."

"You're being deliberately obtuse." I roll my eyes at Quinn's sarcasm. "You understand my meaning, you fucking asshole."

Quinn heaves out a heavy sigh and rubs his hands together. "It's you who's being obtuse. No, you will hear me out," he insists when I try to speak over him again. "Yes, Rapunzel could have helped your father. But you weren't the one locked in a goddamn tower and had it shoved into your brain that you were a danger to the world your whole fucking life. You've known this woman since you were a boy. Think about it, Wren. Do you honestly believe she is so evil that she would sit back and do nothing while your parents suffered? She was more terrified of her power than she was of stepping one foot out of that prison for twenty-four years. Think about that, you pigheaded dick. She's not John, no matter how badly you need to paint them with the same brush."

Fuck Quinn. I don't want to hear this right now.

I assumed he, of all people, would understand my resentment toward Rapunzel. Instead, here he is arguing on her behalf. "Is this the way of it?"

He narrows those fierce eyes at me. "The way of what?"

"You choose that bitch's side over mine?"

Quinn's bitter laugh echoes throughout the empty hall. "You're a fucking fool if you think I would take her *side* over yours. But that doesn't mean I won't call you out when you're wrong. And in this, my friend, you're allowing anger and grief to rule your mind. That will get us killed."

He pushes off the chair and strides out of the hall, leaving me with his warning—and that's precisely what it was, a warning of the inevitable—to question…everything.

Fuck him, and fuck Rapunzel.

Chapter Nineteen

RAPUNZEL

All eyes keep drifting to me. It's unnerving—and irritating. One would think by now their curiosity would be spent. I've been here for two weeks and know each man who calls Dyhurst home. Still, their scrutinizing gazes make me feel like an oddity rather than a person.

Actually, not *all* eyes drift to me.

One person refuses to glance in my direction. Wren keeps his head down, scowl firmly in place, as he shovels food into his face. Tempting as it is to toss a plump apple at his stubborn head, I resist the urge. I wish I could blame his behavior on John having torn through another town, but that would be a lie. To the devil with the grumpy man. If he wants to ruin his meal, that's on him. He'll not spoil mine. Not when I spent much of the afternoon cooking it.

After Arthur and I selected the ripest pickings from the garden, we brought our bounty to the kitchen. There, I helped Bryce—a cantankerous, battle-scarred former soldier who mans the cookfire like the warrior he is—prepare the evening meal. Although he made a big show of acting bothered about having me underfoot, it took little time for him to grudgingly admit we make a good team. Now, it's become a regular occurrence for me to assist him in his precious domain.

It's wonderful to have a purpose.

Exhausted after a day spent working to maintain the castle, I hide a yawn behind my hand. I'm relieved when those curious gazes finally leave me alone. Conversation shifts to John's latest attack on Haversville village. But talk changes fast, and I struggle to keep pace as voices whirl around me. These people care for each other with their easy smiles and playful banter. My heart tugs at the interaction, and I laugh at their bawdy jests. Emma gets right in there with the men, her wit as racy as theirs.

With Wren seated at the head of the long, battered wooden table, it's clear he's the unofficial leader of this motley band of renegades. Dax is at his right, already a bit intoxicated. To his left is Quinn, who repeatedly slides that chilling—and unreadable—gaze over me. Warrick, a former huntsman like Wren, left to bring aid to the recently destroyed village.

If John's army is in the area, it could mean Sybil is also. She might have spread the rumor I'm here, not realizing Wren had taken me and brought me to this remote corner of Rygard. Hope flares in my chest that if I find her, she can help...

...put me right back in a cage.

At least with Wren, my future is unknown. With Sybil, I know what awaits me. Walls. Isolation. A lifetime of loneliness. Her good intentions are more brutal than anything Wren has planned for me.

I glance at my captor and itch to slap the scowl off his flawlessly handsome face. And, as if he reads my thoughts, his mouth kicks up in a sneer, and he gives me a single shake of his head. He whispers something to Quinn, who lifts a black brow, his devious grin sending a warm flush to my cheeks.

They've left me alone this past fortnight, with Dax stealing kisses here and there as I've settled into my newfound freedom. But I've sensed a growing tension whenever he, Wren, and

Quinn look at me. Their tension is a brewing storm. One that's slowly whipping me into a frenzy, their eyes reminding me of the pleasure they're capable of bringing me.

This castle may be a decaying shell, but it *is* still a fortress, complete with a fully functioning gate. There is always someone stationed on the parapet keeping a watchful eye. And, as Bryce warned me while pointing a battered spoon in my face, I'd best not run. Quinn will find me.

'God save you then, lass.'

Emma, bless her, is my lifeline throughout the rest of the meal. She sits next to me, maintaining a steady chatter as the men's voices boom around us. Until Ian roars my name. The burly knight, with his unruly blonde hair and scarred hands and arms, seems a storied man whose body tells of his battles.

"You've yet to tell us how you like our humble home?" Ian's gravelly voice carries across the table and quiets the din of conversation. Wren keeps his focus to his plate while everyone else watches me. I wish the freshly swept stone floor would open and swallow me as I bristle under the unwanted attention.

There is nothing humble about Dyhurst. Surely the small castle desperately needs repair, but in its glory, it must have been grand indeed.

"I like it fine." My hand tightens around the fork until the metal bites into my sweaty palm. I wonder if the day will come when I'll grow comfortable speaking to a group without my stomach aching—or not wanting to cringe at the sound of my voice.

He nods at Emma. "I'm sure our sister is pleased to have reinforcements."

Sister. The endearment from such a rugged man makes it even more meaningful.

Emma throws a chunk of bread at Ian. "You got that right, you big brute."

With his massive arms and broad chest, he has surprisingly

quick reflexes. He catches the bread and takes a big bite. "You'd be lost without us."

She gives the gruff man a shy smile. "More like you'd be lost without me."

"Aye, lady, we would."

Is he blushing?

Is she?

Oh my, they are.

How adorable.

Now that I watch them, I wonder if either realizes how they can barely keep their eyes off each other without flushing and getting flustered. Emma is suddenly fidgeting in her chair. Ian has a wistful curve to his scarred upper lip. They both seem to pretend they're not attracted to each other by swiftly letting the moment pass. Already I'm playing matchmaker in my mind...

Lucian, a young and handsome warrior with clipped red hair and a tidy beard, asks about my life. Although there isn't much to tell given that I don't have grand stories like my battle-worn companions, they hang on my every word as I take them through my life in the tower. I keep it simple, explaining how Sybil traveled across Rygard to spread those false rumors to thwart anyone who might know of my existence. How, in her chronic absence, I painted my walls and read hundreds of books. What I don't tell them, what I keep only for myself, is how I gazed out the window for hours at a stretch, imagining a world I believed I'd never experience.

How I stared at the ground and contemplated jumping to my death.

Wondered if I *could* die or if my hair would protect me. But always, I was too much of a coward to spare myself a lifetime of misery, hidden away—Rygard's dirty secret.

My guilt over not saving Wren's father stays locked in my heart. I don't tell them how I wept for weeks after Wren stormed off that day. How I didn't eat or drink or sleep as I skated along the edge of madness. It was in those darkest moments that I tried. Oh, God, I tried to end it. And that's when I learned the magic does, indeed, protect its vessel.

It will not let me get sick.

It will not allow me to die.

As long as the magic infects my hair, it infuses my body with health.

With life.

I shove my plate away. Dax notices I haven't finished my food and remarks about me being too frail. He claims I need to eat more. Tristan counters this by saying I'm fine as I am. Dax whips back that they're simply worried I won't survive a harsh Dyhurst winter. Gavin grumbles that children are dying of starvation due to John taxing the people of Rygard literally to death, and they need to start gathering supplies for distribution once the weather turns.

Wren's hostile eyes fry me from across the table. "Rapunzel doesn't give a fuck about the dying."

His cruel statement hits me like a winter storm, instantly cooling the lingering heat of his glare. I clasp my trembling hands because if I don't, I fear I'll do something outrageous—like slap him across his smug face. I believe I've been tolerant, more than generous, given what he's lost. But Wren has no right to torment me to assuage his pain. I've had enough.

"Please excuse me." I shove away from the table.

Emma is already halfway out of her chair, but I press her back down with a gentle hand on her shoulder. "Are you unwell?"

Scowling, I drag my gaze from Wren and offer Emma a false, reassuring shake of my head. "I'm tired, that's all." Then I cast a look over the assortment of renegades who are watching me as I stand. "I'm fine, truly."

I'm simply annoyed and have no wish to suffer Wren's irritating presence.

"Thank God for your help in the kitchen," Gavin calls out as I walk away from the table. It's difficult to imagine the dark-haired knight having worn John's colors, given how he literally spits every time he hears the king's name. I can't blame him. When he refused to commit atrocities for John, the king ordered him beaten to the point that he now walks with a limp. "I speak for all of us when I admit we were growing tired of Bryce's bland stews."

Bryce doesn't pause from shoveling his meal into his maw. "To the devil with you."

Quinn's fork clatters against his metal plate. Everyone halts to stare at the doomed man. It's easy to forget the devil is not an abstract entity for Quinn. After studying Bryce for what seems like endless tense moments, he sighs. "Sorry, but no. We don't want him there." He picks up his fork, spears a carrot, and holds it to his mouth. "Although his stew should guarantee him a spot."

The tension dissipates as everyone piles on the harmless ribbing of Bryce's culinary skills. But it leaves me with the realization that Quinn *will* be reborn as a demon as part of his bargain when he surrendered his soul.

This day has been long, and this meal is suddenly endless. Emma calls out to me when I reach the first step and reminds me that she's only a chamber away if I need anything. Her friendship reassures me, and when I walk toward the stairs, I do it with a light heart even as Wren's rancor burns me as I march toward the safety of my chamber.

I trudge up the steep dimly lit steps leading to the keep's upper level. And once I reach my room, I'm grateful for the fire in the hearth. Even in summer, castle walls hold a damp chill. It's nice that someone thought to do this kindness for me.

I peel off the green tunic. It's a bit loose, but I'm grateful for the trunk of clothing Dax graciously provided for me. I didn't ask where the clothing came from when he brought it to me the day after we arrived. He simply set it at the foot of the bed and followed it with a kiss that left me breathless.

I drape the gold-trimmed gown over the chair near the arrow slit of a window, then kick off my sturdy, brown boots. After I strip away the delicate white chemise, I use the tepid water in a basin resting in the corner of the room to wash as best I can.

Tomorrow, I plan to have a proper bath in the copper tub—and if Wren grumbles about it again, too damn bad.

I tug on a new chemise and settle under the cool, crisp blanket. After a full day's worth of activity, it feels wonderful to lay my body at rest. It takes no time at all for me to slip into sleep…

…until I'm pulled right back out by the door creaking open. The ancient hinges groan, whipping me awake. I jolt up, and in the faint firelight, I see the large outline of Wren unlacing his shirt.

Momentarily struck dumb, I gawk like a fool. I stupidly watch him peel off his shirt and gape at his sun-kissed skin. Marvel at the sheer breadth of his shoulders. And when he turns his back on me… My God. It's a struggle to stifle a gasp at the crisscrossed lash scars that mar his flesh. Who would dare harm him? Even as the question forms, a prominent name follows in its wake.

John.

But why? Much of Wren's life is a mystery, and as I snap out of my stupor, I wish… I wish for many things. That I could undo my choices to make him…*un*hate…me because I miss his friendship. Miss his laugh. His silly jests. How he worried I would tumble from the tower when I would sit on the ledge and dangle my leg over the side.

Mostly, I miss his love.

When he took that from me, he took my heart as well. Left an aching hollow in the center of my world.

"Why are you in my room?"

He tosses the shirt on the chair and turns to face me. "Your room?" Wren's face may be cast in shadow, but I see the sneer that curls his upper lip just fine. "Fucking presumptuous of you."

"Fine, it's not my room." I hike the blanket to my chin as if he hasn't already seen me naked. "But you're allowing me to use it. Please leave."

He stalks toward the bed as he removes his sword. Then takes care to wrap the straps of the belt around the sheath. He leans the weapon against the wall where he can easily reach it before working the laces of his breeches.

I panic. "What are you doing?"

"How else do you expect me to remove them?" His sarcastic tone bounces off the stone walls.

I give him a firm shake of my head. "No, Wren."

His hands go still, his expression cold. "No?"

"No." I notch my chin. "You can't sleep in this bed."

My God, but must he look so smug? "You realize this is my goddamn room." His hands get busy again until the last lace falls open. He shucks his boots. Shimmies those brown breeches over his hips, and I want to look away. Lord knows I do, but I don't. I can't. Or maybe I simply won't. I sit there, the blanket still ridiculously hiked high, and I watch as he slowly—so slowly—slides his pants down his long, muscular legs. The light dusting of hair does nothing to take away from the sun-kissed perfection of his body.

A body I wondered what looked like naked for years.

Dreamed about.

I imagined touching when I was alone in the dark, my hands on my own body, pretending we were together.

But he was always too far out of reach. And now he's here. Close enough that if I extend my arm, my fingers will brush over his taut abdomen. Yet he seems farther away from me now than ever when I was in that tower.

This cruel reality would break my heart if he hadn't already shattered it.

Wren flips the blanket, forcing me to grip it tighter to keep it from snapping free from my hold. When he climbs onto the mattress, he keeps to his side as if I'm so disgusting, no part of him can even graze me.

"If you despise me, why are you here?"

He settles under the blanket, and I think he won't answer me. But then he does, his gruff voice cutting through the silence. "I fought too hard to get this far. You're not worth one more night spent sleeping on the goddamn floor in the hall." Then he sighs, the sound...pained. "I thought this would be easy, having you here." He pauses, and I think he's done complaining. He's not, and his admission levels me. "I was wrong."

His honesty is raw, and I smile into the dark as if I achieved a small victory. But I know I've gained nothing at all.

"Fine." I toss off the blanket and sit up. Before my feet hit the floor, I'm hauled back on the bed and staring up at Wren. He hovers over me like impending doom. I want to smooth that mess of brown hair away from his scowling face. Run my fingertips along his lips. See something other than hostility in his intrusive brown eyes.

But I do none of those things. Instead, I keep my hands fisted at my sides, with his animosity a barrier between us.

"I didn't tell you to leave."

"I don't recall asking for your permission." My entire body sags with frustration. "What do you want from me, Wren?"

"I don't know," he admits, clearly annoyed—at me. Maybe even at himself.

I finally succumb to temptation and cup his face. The contact is electric. "I won't be your villain. I'll be anything for you but that because I can't—*I won't*—have you hate me."

His eyes close, but only for a moment. When they reopen, they're filled with so much pain that it shreds my heart. "Why, Rapunzel? Why didn't you help him?"

"I'm sorry," I breathe, shifting my hold on him to run my

hands through his hair. But he rolls away to lie on his back. I can't see much, but I don't need to. His agony flows over me in violent waves. "Wren, please—"

"Just go to sleep, Rapunzel." For once, there isn't an edge to his voice. No, not this time. There is only...torment.

I wish I were made of different magic. The kind that could bring us back to the day I refused to go to my window when I heard his call. Because I would live that day so very differently. I would ignore a lifetime of fear and risk Rygard—risk everything —to save Wren's father. Because that day, I did nothing. I hid. From Wren—and from myself. I've regretted that decision every moment since.

That day, I earned Wren's hatred, and it's a hatred that is well deserved.

I turn away from him, giving him my back to hide my shame. But the mattress dips with his movements, and his arms come around me. He hauls me against his chest. Cradles me into the crook of his body. I can't breathe. Can't think. I can only...*feel*.

Feel Wren's hard body behind me.

Each deep and steady breath he draws.

My heart beats an erratic rhythm as my dreams of this moment become a reality. My breath shudders, and I squeeze my eyes closed to hold back tears. Wren can claim to hate me, and I can hate myself, but all that melts away under the cover of darkness. It leaves just...us...and as I drift into sleep, I cling to this moment, wishing I could hold onto this night forever, even as it slips through my fingers like the dirt he once crumbled when I asked him what the dirt felt like beneath his feet.

Chapter Twenty

QUINN

My instincts are never wrong.

Warrick's four-day absence warned me something was amiss. Fuck me if my soulless self wasn't right. As I weave my steed through the carnage left behind in the wake of John's most recent attack on Rygard, I damn near choke on the stench of death permeating the air.

This... This is senseless slaughter. None of it was necessary. John is more powerful than one man has a right to be. He doesn't need Rapunzel. But need and want are synonymous to a man drunk on hubris.

Good people died here. Innocent lives wasted. Women and children, murdered along with the men. I shouldn't care. I don't *want* to care. But when I close my eyes against the gruesome scene, the terrible evil that lingers fills the emptiness left behind in the space my soul once inhabited.

My eyes fly open when I detect the faintest rumble of male voices. At the surge of bloodlust, the dark energy inside me spikes. I bring my steed to a stop and slip off its back. I have my sword palmed before my feet touch the ground. Following the sound, I creep silently through the burnt-out village. Past skeletal buildings and rotting corpses, until I come upon two soldiers pillaging the remnants of the blacksmith's hut.

Fucking grave robbers, that's what they are, masquerading as royal cavalry. They rummage through damaged weaponry, searching for whatever is salvageable, with the artisan's charred body lying among the rubble.

Foolish bastards. They should have left with the others, because when I'm done here, there'll be two more dead in the debris.

"Found one." The younger soldier holds up a soot-covered sword. He twirls the weapon in his gauntleted hand, showing it to his companion.

"Looks good." The other man removes his helmet and shakes out his red hair. He squints his blue eyes and inspects the impressive sword. "I claim it."

"Fuck off. I found it." The blonde soldier tucks it behind his back like a petulant child. "That makes it mine." Then he nods at a small scattering of swords half-buried under scorched straw. "There's more over there, but I'm not moving him to get them."

Him being the blacksmith.

"Squeamish, that's what you are," Red grumbles. "If you won't do it, I will, and I'll keep the fortune we'll get selling them to those knights-errant in Loslow."

"If they're still there by the time we get back up north." The blonde is still examining the sword, too smug for his own good. "We could try selling them in Leighton Falls. Although we scared those skittish folks something fierce when we marched through there waving the king's standard."

"Aye, we did." Red puffs up proudly—the fucking prick. "Nothing like the power of the crown to frighten lesser men."

There is no power on Rygard's throne. Nor is there power in this hut. There are only two scavengers who are a blight upon humanity.

Everything within me demands I kill them slow. Make it

hurt. But I hold myself in check and watch as the blonde places the finely crafted sword across the cold forge. He snickers, picking through the debris as Red marches toward the blacksmith and grabs the dead man's arms. I grit my teeth against a wave of fury as Red hauls the body across the hut, pulling it over rubble as if the man were trash.

The disrespect is irritating but not surprising. In John's court, honor is a wasted word. His courtiers don't dare turn their backs on each other for fear of getting a dagger stabbed between their shoulder blades. The garrison is a pack of heathens with little training. They're plucked from the trenches of Rygard, handed a sword, a tabard emblazoned with John's standard, and unleashed upon the kingdom. As much as I want to rip their souls from their bodies, these miserable lumps of pig shit aren't worth the pain and energy it would cost me.

Instead, I inch inside the hut, weapon at the ready, and intrude on their little pillage party. "Hate to interrupt. However, I would advise against touching one more fucking thing in this village."

Red stops dragging the blacksmith and drops the dead man's arms. He blinks at me once, twice, before it registers that someone would dare interfere with their looting. "Get a load of this one's audacity." He jabs a thumb at his companion, emboldened by the apparent misconception that I'm outmanned. "Have at him, Osric."

Osric, the fool, pulls his sword from its sheath. It's the last thing he does. I have no time for games and make quick work of opening a deep gash across his abdomen.

His intestines spill at his feet.

Glorious.

Stunned by the speed and force of my attack, Osric drops his weapon. He clutches his disemboweled body, futilely trying to stuff himself back inside the cavity. I would hang him from a tree by his entrails if I had more time, but unfortunately, I don't.

Twisted

Instead, I grunt out a disgusted laugh and kick him backward. He slips in his mess and lands on his back. His eyes roll in their sockets, and he gargles on a mouthful of blood.

With blade in one hand, I hover it over the man's chest. In my peripheral, I see Red charge for me. Brave fucker. I stay focused on the felled soldier and, quick as a blink, extend my left arm. My hand clamps around Red's throat. I lift him off his feet and dangle him like a doll. I finally give him my full attention, relishing the sight of him gasping for breath. Then I carry him across the hut. A cloud of soot puffs out from behind him when I slam his back against the nearest wall—hard enough to crack the scorched timber.

I bare my teeth in a snarl. "You're regretting your entire life right about now, aren't you?"

His terrified gaze searches my face. I know what he sees when he looks into my eyes.

The promise of pain.

So much pain.

"What are you?"

I draw back my arm. Plunge my blade so deep into his chest, it pierces the wall. Red gasps. His eyes bulge. He glances down, sees my sword protruding from his body, then slowly drags his gaze back to my face.

"I'm a fucking monster." I pull free my sword. He lands with a thud on the debris-strewn floor, barely alive and sucking in labored breaths. Hands over his bleeding chest, he stares up at me, but I'm already done with him. I glance at Osric and crook a grin when I see he's dead in a mess of bowels. His empty eyes stare back at me. Good. I was the last thing the prick saw before death took him. And when I shift my gaze back at Red, I shake my head as I watch him attempt to level his weapon at me. "Noble effort, but foolish. And futile."

I kick the sword out of his hand.

"Fuck you." He spits at my feet.

Sneering, I place my booted foot on his chest, directly over his wound. I step down, putting enough weight on him to crush bone. His howl of agony sings throughout the hut. "Save a place in hell for your king."

With my need to find Warrick paramount in my mind, I'm already thinking ten steps ahead. Focused on where I'm going to—

"Hello, Quinn."

If it were anyone else but *him* behind me, I would have detected the threat. But this motherfucker always threw me off balance. That's the way of it, I suppose, when you once trusted someone with your whole self.

Goddamn it.

Eventually, our paths would cross. This day had to happen, same as day follows night. I've been waiting for it—I just assumed I would be prepared when it did. Fuck me, but I was wrong. And when I whip around, ready to strike, every muscle in my body freezes at the sight of Sir Stephan of Glasburg.

The fucker strolls inside the ruined hut as if he's striding into a palace. I want to rip the smug expression clean off his face.

"Look at you, dressed up in the king's colors." I sniff the air. "But fuck, you stink like you crawled out of his ass."

Stephan casts his cold, blue gaze at the carnage. "At home among the dead, I see."

I lift a brow, my grip tightening around the hilt of my sword. "I'll gladly add one more body to the count."

"I'm sure you would, my friend." His nasty laugh grates across my nerves.

"We were *never* friends."

"Weren't we?" Stephan *tsks* me. "Did we not grow up together? Were we not as close as brothers?" He steps toward me, and I raise my arm, leveling my sword at his black fucking heart. "Did I not keep my promise to elevate your family name?"

I should rip Stephan's tongue from his mouth for that remark.

I step over Red's body, destroying more of the distance separating me from a man I once loved like family. "You served only yourself."

Stephan shrugs, and his apathy—his greed—feeds the dark power flowing through my veins. "We do what we must to survive in John's kingdom. You, of all people, should understand this."

"I've become this *thing* because of you!" My roar rocks the foundation of the hut.

The blast of fury sends Stephan back a few steps. He releases a sad sigh, but his eyes remain as cold as a winter's day. "No, Quinn. You surrendered your soul because you were too stubborn to accept that I did what was best for all of us."

Fury clouds my vision. Pushed too far, I charge Stephan. I propel him backward until he hits the wall. Slam my forearm against his throat. Use that pressure to pin him in place. "John wanted a pretty, young bride, so you gave him Eleanor. You traded your betrothed to sit at the head of the king's army. You have no care that he beats her. That he abuses her—*my sister*. All you care about is power. But I have power now, too, Stephan, you narcissistic bastard."

"He swore he would treat her well." He struggles to speak against the stress I'm putting on his throat. Tries to pry my arm away, but my strength far outmatches his.

"You never believed that." I press harder, cutting off whatever excuses he might try to make for what he's done to my family. "You're many things, but stupid isn't among them."

"You can't win this, Quinn," Stephan grinds out. "John is powerful. You're…one man. Against the royal…army."

With a humorless laugh, I sheath my sword. I offer him a cruel smile and flex my fingers. "I'll show you power, Stephan, unlike anything you've ever seen."

He must realize my intentions because he brokenly babbles for me to wait. Pleading, between gasps, to grant him time so he can explain. That he had only wished for the good of our families' futures when he brought Eleanor to court and presented her to John. She was seventeen, and within weeks of their wedding, I received the first letter—the parchment stained with her blood.

The king was...hurting her.

She begged me to bring her home.

I told my father, but the fucker was too busy counting his newly acquired fortune to care.

Stephan's pleas for his life are a distant echo in my ears. Barely audible above the memory of my sister's cries.

I take a deep, calming breath before I plunge my hand into Stephan's chest. My fingers tear through flesh and muscle. Crack bone and snap tendons. When I reach his heart, I grip it, wet and beating, and rip it from its cavity.

My movements are so fast and violent his mind remains conscious when I hold his heart up for him to see. Rivulets of blood stream down my arm when I look him dead in the eyes and drag my tongue over the warm organ. I savor his coppery taste. Then I grab his chin and hold his head captive.

"Your life is over, but your pain has just begun."

Once I meet him in hell, I'll have eternity to test the limits of my creativity torturing him. He deserves nothing less for the evil he brought down on my sister.

Watching him die, as exquisite as it is, distracts me. Fuck. The attack catches me by surprise. Stabbed in the back, I drop Stephan's heart and grab my sword. As I spin, I'm struck again, sliced across the face. Blinded by pain and blood, I stumble backward and land on my ass. I count three men. No, two, I correct myself when I blink away the thick, stinging wet that floods my eyes. I shake my head, struggling to clear my vision. Two men shouldn't be a problem...

...except it is, because my mind is muddy and when I try to push myself to my feet... I stumble and flop back down. My arms are too heavy, my limbs disjointed. I fight to regain my footing, and as each moment passes, it's as if more weight gets added to my body. More fog clouds my mind.

"The fuck have you done to me?" My words are slurred at the soldier standing over me.

"This is the legendary Quinn Redgrave?" He points at me, laughing. "Not so fearsome now, are you?"

I turn my head to the right to see my sword lying useless on the floor, out of reach. I refocus my blurred vision on the men. One of them levels a sword at me, the blade coated with black ooze.

"Poison? Have you any idea how many fools have tried that on me?" My sneer comes out more of a croak as whatever they used on me slithers through my body.

The second soldier comes into focus, his brown hair greasy around a dirty face. Rotted teeth are exposed when his mouth stretches into a crooked grin. "But the king's new toy didn't make their poisons like she did this one."

"Shut your mouth." The taller man elbows him. "No one's supposed to know about the witch."

The witch?

Fuck.

"Does it matter, Justin?" The soldier gestures at me. "Look at him. He's as good as dead." Then he leans in close—but not too close. "Those eyes. Black as sin, they are. It's true then. You really gave your soul to the devil?"

A demon, but far be it from me to correct this asshole.

"John..." I struggle to form words. "Has a witch?"

"Damn right he does." The man nods. "Our liege keeps her locked up tight. Rumor has it her screams echo throughout Newkirk Castle."

Sybil.

Her name whispers across my mind. It has to be her. I don't need to hear them say it aloud for confirmation. I *feel* her in the poison. Now that John has her and he's torturing her, he'll get her to tell him everything about Rapunzel—if he hasn't already.

Goddamn fuck.

I've witnessed firsthand the level of suffering that prick can inflict on a person. It's why I sacrificed everything to save my sister. I always believed I'd find a way to use this power to defeat John and free Eleanor from him.

That hope dies with me, today.

So does Rapunzel's future.

One soldier kicks me, and I try to hold back my howl of pain. There's laughter. Taunts. Then the tainted blade drags across my throat, slow and deep. Agony spreads like a wildfire from my gaping throat to every part of me. It picks at my nerves as my blood seeps from the wound. Thick and sticky, it fills my mouth. Chokes me. Skids down my throat, only to bleed back out.

"That should finish him."

They're not wrong, as I go as still as death.

"Finally." He spits on me. "Fucking abomination."

The darkness pulls me in, leaving me vulnerable. I can't avoid slipping into it like sliding into a lake of lava. This journey is unbearable. It's pain in its purest form. There's no escape from it—and I see him in this darkness. The demon, with his black eyes and evil grin. He beckons to me. Eager to begin whatever it is he has planned for me…

But the unmistakable sound of an arrow cutting through the air snaps me out of the darkness. It strikes true, piercing the soldier with the sword in the throat. The weapon clamors to the floor with a metallic clang that vibrates against my aching bones. A second shot impales the other man in the chest but doesn't kill him.

Wren rushes in and grabs the sword. Then his face fills my vision. "You're a fucking mess." His flippant remark doesn't match the concern etched across his face.

"Witch poison." The words are a coarse whisper.

My tendons try to stitch themselves together, but the venom destroys faster. I want to laugh at the realization that all my dark power is doing is prolonging my suffering—and my imminent death—instead of healing me.

Wren closes his eyes for a moment—just a single moment. Then he glances at the ooze smeared across the blade. "You better not die on me."

That's one promise I can't make. "Swear to me. You won't. Blame Rapunzel."

Those words cost almost too much energy.

"I won't." He shoves his hair away from his furrowed brow, revealing a faint cringe he can't hide. "But if you die, she'll blame herself, so you better survive this because I won't comfort her."

If I could laugh at his stubbornness, I would.

And yes, he would comfort her, the fool. Wren loves her. He's always loved her. But now, despite myself, I care about the woman as well. So does Dax. For the first time since I sold my soul, I have something more to live for other than revenge. I don't want my life to end here, on this floor, but Sybil's poison isn't leaving me a choice.

My traitorous blood rushes from my wounds as if in a frenzy to escape this condemned body. The poison is a slow river of fire spreading through me as I struggle to tell Wren what happened here. About Stephan, because it's important he knows. I catch fragments of the surviving soldier's confession and my fucking heart breaks as I watch Wren kill the bastard with Sybil's tainted sword. Then the demon is there, in the dark, waiting for me.

This time he's not smiling.

Maybe he finally realizes that when he bartered for my soul, he acquired something far darker and more feral than he could control.

Either way, in the end, we're both fucked.

Chapter Twenty-One

DAX

"Good morning, Little Captive."

"That's not nice, Dax." Rapunzel rolls her eyes at my remark as I stroll inside Wren's chamber. I come bearing gifts. Then her expression changes to confusion. "Wren isn't here. Did he not tell you he was leaving to help at Haversville?"

Of course he did.

Last evening, Wren got it in his stubborn head to follow Quinn. He left me to watch over Rapunzel. Not a problem. There are worse duties than seeing to the safety of our little enchanted prisoner.

Which is one of the reasons I'm interrupting her bath...

I inhale the subtle aroma of roses as I cross the room, and when I reach the tub, I see delicate red petals floating in the water around Rapunzel's flawless body. She does nothing to cover her modesty, and goddamn but I envy Wren. He has the luxury of sleeping beside her, which I suppose is fair. He's known her since they were children, and no matter if he admits it or not, he loves her.

Twisted

"Now, why would I come searching for that ornery asshole when you're here wearing my favorite outfit?"

She scrunches her face, her nose wrinkling. A little laugh escapes her pink lips. "I'm not wearing anything at all, Dax."

"Exactly." I hold up the bundle in my arms. "But also, I bring treasure."

Rapunzel's lovely green eyes light with joy. "For me?"

I snort out a laugh. "It's certainly not for Wren."

She tilts her head and regards me curiously. "Why?"

"What? Bring you gifts?" Walking to the bed, I drop my bounty on the mattress. When I turn back around, I catch her nod. "Because I like you." Too much, I silently add. I stroll to the tub with her gaze on me and I feel it like a physical touch. "Let me help you out of there, my lady, before you catch your death."

She flips a lock of her damp hair. "Impossible." Her playful wink is nothing short of captivating. "And you haven't known me long enough to like me. For all you know, Wren could be correct about me being an awful person."

Worse, I feat that *she* believes it.

When she extends her hands, I grip them, marveling at how everything about her is graceful. "Rapunzel, you've allowed other people's words to infect your mind." I lift her from the water, transfixed for a moment, as I watch droplets of water slide over the lovely curves of her body. "Seems I have a difficult task of convincing you that you're not the monster Sybil would have you believe you are."

She averts her eyes sheepishly. "You can try."

I grab a towel and wrap it around her, then help her out of the tub. "I'm quite persuasive."

Rapunzel puts up a weak protest while I dry her. The stubborn woman even slaps my hands away. But I'm bigger and stronger and a born warrior. I also prove my argument about being persuasive when she eventually relents. Smugly, I accept this victory, and when I'm satisfied I've dried every drop of water from her incredible body—while wishing my tongue was the towel—I select a cream chemise from the trunk of clothing at the foot of the bed.

After I help Rapunzel into the garment, I lead her to the bed and point to the wrapped bundle sitting in the center of the mattress. "Figured you would appreciate more enjoyable ways to pass the time than listening to Wren's grumbles."

"You didn't have to do this." She gestures to the chemise. To the trunk. "I need nothing." Then she gestures to the chamber. "Freedom from the tower was gift enough."

"Freedom is well and good." I kick up a brow, one corner of my mouth lifting in a grin. "But the clothes were a necessity. You would have caused quite the scandal if you were to run around Dyhurst naked." I smooth my hands down her sides. Pull her against me and trail kisses along the column of her throat. "I've never wanted a woman the way I crave you."

"It's the magic, Dax." The silly woman has no idea how captivating she is—hair be damned. "Not me."

I shake my head. Slide my tongue along her lips until she opens for me. Lick my way inside and fuck her mouth, my blood rushing to my cock until it strains against my breeches. Until the beast between my legs damn near rips through the laces, demanding release.

I could spend the rest of the day lost in her, but that would defeat the purpose of why I'm here. Reluctantly, I break the kiss and set Rapunzel at arm's distance. "Open it." I ache to toss her on the bed and be the first to feel the hug of her body around my cock, but I refrain. Wren better appreciate the discipline it takes for me to release her.

Rapunzel touches a fingertip to her lips. Hesitantly, she empties the sack—and gasps. Gasps at the collection of books, ribbons, jars of paint, and brushes. I'd decorate her in jewels, but I won't spend frivolously. Not when we put our gold to better use

Twisted

buying food and supplies for suffering Rygardians. Yet seeing the joy on her face makes the expense well worth it.

"Dax..." She touches each item with reverence. Picks up a book, cracks it open, and trails a finger down a random page. She whispers Latin words with ease. On her tongue, the lyrical words are poetry written directly by God's hand. She could recite a recipe for cockentrice, and I wouldn't know it, but I'd listen to her read it for hours. After carefully closing the book, she inspects the other simple gifts as if they are the finest treasures. Then she turns to me, and I puff with pride under the glow of her joy. "Thank you."

On someone else's tongue, those words would sound simple. The emotion she puts in them hits me like a punch to my gut. "You're welcome, Rapunzel."

She takes a step toward me. Then another. Laces her fingers through mine. "May I kiss you this time, Dax, rather than *you* kiss *me*?"

Goddamn this woman.

"Anywhere and everywhere you please, Little Captive." I place my free hand over my heart. "I am yours."

Rapunzel's lips part as she closes what little space there is between us. She releases my hands and wraps her arms around my neck. It takes all I have to allow her to take the lead. She's hesitant, but once she presses her mouth to mine, she breathes a soft sigh and melts into me. Moves to my throat, where her lips ignite an inferno everywhere they touch. Then she's back to my mouth, her chaste kiss achingly tender.

"There's more to your gift," I whisper against her lips. Then I lean away and kiss the tip of her nose. "Finish dressing, lovely Rapunzel, for today, I take you on an adventure."

Her eyes light with excitement and she claps her hands. "Truly?"

"Truly," I confirm with a wink.

She rushes into a blue tunic. I help her tie a belt of golden thread around her trim waist. Then I spend an ungodly amount of time brushing her hair. Rather than plait the heavy mass, I pick a yellow ribbon from the batch I bought her and wrap it around the blonde waves.

She tugs on her boots, and we're off. Down the steep steps to the hall. Whatever Bryce is roasting in the kitchen smells divine, and I can bet my balls that sometime today, Rapunzel will head there to help with the meal. Thank God. She'll fatten us up in no time if she keeps feeding us such splendid meals. But she won't join Bryce straightaway. First, she'll help Arthur in the garden. But not before her daily conversation with Kenric. Then, of course, she'll visit with Emma for a bit. Then after, she'll make her rounds checking on Ian and Gavin, and Tristan and Lucian. Because Rapunzel may have been in Dyhurst for only a short time, but already she made this castle her home and our people her family.

If that's not magic, I don't know what is.

~

"Tell me about yourself."

"There's not much to know." I shrug at Rapunzel's statement as we stroll along the cliff's edge.

Was it a risk to take her beyond Dyhurst's walls? Yes. But it was a calculated one. The castle sits on a peninsula with a single land passage by way of approach. Neither Wren nor I found any disturbance in the surrounding area that would alert us of a threat to our rugged and secluded corner of Rygard. She deserves a few stolen moments outside the castle walls for a better view of the sea.

Rapunzel tucks stray hair behind her ear, much of the golden mass wind-blown out of the ribbon. "Then it shouldn't take long to tell me everything."

Cheeky wench.

Twisted

"I'm not a complex person. My father was a knight-errant. Whenever he passed through Lansing, he'd visit my mother at her tavern, The Cup and Crown." I cut her a droll stare when I see her optimistic expression. "Get those silly thoughts out of your pretty head, Rapunzel. It's not a love story. I'm a bastard in the truest sense. My sire ran off to chase fortune, glory, and adventure. We met one time, when I was a boy. We wouldn't recognize each other if we met on the battlefield. He could be dead by now for all I know."

Or care.

She gives my hand a reassuring squeeze. "I'm sorry you never knew him."

"I'm not." I think of how Adele Stafford fought for respectability in a man's world. "My mother worked hard to give me a good life."

Rapunzel stares at the Lennox Sea, watching the violent waves rip over the surface. They batter the cliff, with the wind whipping her golden hair around her lithe body. I swear, in this moment, against the harsh beauty of southern Rygard, she's a goddess among men.

"You were lucky, Dax."

The sorrow in her voice fucking kills me.

"She's mean as hell." My mother had to be or this kingdom would have chewed her up and spit her out. "But yes, she's a wonderful woman. One day you'll meet her, and she'll adore you."

When Rapunzel fixes her gaze on me, I swear it makes the world drop away, leaving only the two of us. Even the roar of the sea fades as I drown in those captivating green eyes. "Why did you become a knight?"

"I suppose, along with being Adele Stafford's son, I also have Sir Simon Baines's blood flowing through my veins."

She draws her brows in a perplexed frown. "You haven't taken your father's surname."

I point to myself. "Bastard, remember?" I offer her a lopsided grin. "Baines never openly claimed me as his own."

"That's... That's a horrible thing for a father to do."

"Rapunzel, it's fine." Her outrage is adorable, if not misplaced. "I harbor no ill will against the man, nor should you on my behalf." I glance at the sky and note the position of the sun. "Now, look your fill of the sea. It's time we get back inside the walls."

She heaves out a forlorn sigh and nods. "Of course."

After a few moments, I tug her away from the cliff. She drags her feet beside me as if she's carrying the world's weight on her slender shoulders. And I suppose she is. The burden of Rygard must be heavy. Fucking John. Because everything isn't enough for the prick. He wants more. He wants everything.

I watched him take while I served him first as a page, then as a squire, and lastly as a knight. He quietly seized land from the neighboring kingdoms that border Rygard. Claimed the wives of his courtiers—and covertly murdered their husbands if they opposed being a cuckold. Demanded his noblemen raise their sons as his soldiers. Executed dissenting voices to mask his cruelty.

And he did this with a charming grin.

But John couldn't hide behind that false charismatic demeanor forever. His need for power overrode his desire to be loved, and his true nature revealed itself. Now, the good people of Rygard see their king for who he is—a madman devoid of morals.

As Rapunzel and I stroll hand in hand toward Dyhurst, I keep a watchful eye on the landscape. To the west, east, and south is the sea, guarded by ragged cliffs. That leaves the north, but walking up from behind the castle, I don't have a clear view of that area. When we come around to the front, though, I skid to a stop.

Fuck.

On alert, I pull free my sword and shove Rapunzel behind me. "Stay silent."

Horse tracks batter the ground. They lead to the open gate. No one inside would dare drop our defenses to a stranger.

Other than Rapunzel and me, three other inhabitants left Dyhurst.

Warrick.

Wren.

Quinn.

I look back at the horse tracks and mutter another curse when I note the drops of blood in the trampled dirt.

A cold sweat forms on my brow, and my heart drops to my feet when I see Wren slide off his steed—leaving me with a clear view of Quinn lying prone on the saddle. "Fuck."

"What's wrong?" Rapunzel's question sounds distant as a hundred horrific scenarios collide in my mind.

And when I answer her, one word drops from my tongue. One name. "Quinn." I break into a run, dragging Rapunzel with me.

Chapter Twenty-Two

RAPUNZEL

Dax and I enter Dyhurst's courtyard and run straight into chaos.

Someone slams the gate closed behind us. I think I hear the long wooden bar slide into the iron slats of the lock, but I'm not sure because there's too much noise. Everyone is shouting, with the men demanding to know what happened. Emma backs away from the anarchy, her hands covering her mouth. But her eyes... They're wide with horror. None of this makes sense. Dax pries his fingers from mine, and I watch in a daze as he races toward the havoc. I reach out for him but grasp only air. Maybe I even call his name, but I'm unsure of anything.

All I do know is that there's blood everywhere. Wren is soaked in it.

Things slowly crystalize, and my first instinct is to rip a chunk of hair from my scalp to help him. My mind starts to clear, and I realize he's on his feet and barking orders at everyone. That would mean he's not injured. Right? I repeat this to myself at least a dozen times in rapid succession, with my feet stuck in the dirt, unable to move. Scared that if I go to him, he'll reject me, and right now, with my heart in my throat, his hostility will shatter me into a hundred shards of glass.

At Wren's orders, the men whip into action. They help Dax lift something that's strewn across the saddle. Something bloody —which explains Wren's grisly condition. I assume it's an animal. Of course it is. Wren hunts. But no. This is wrong. He'd not be saturated in blood. Nor would Emma be crying. Kenric wouldn't be praying. And why is Bryce threatening to tear down Newkirk Castle to get to John? Everything is still a jumble of motion and noise, and as I try to piece it together...

...I see him.

He's what's draped over Wren's saddle.

Oh, God.

Quinn.

Dax, along with Ian, Tristan, and Gavin, gently lay him on the ground. He's bleeding from... I don't know where because there's so much blood. I'm afraid to get close. Afraid he's dead. The possibility is horrifying. But at his grunt when they peel away his jerkin, I choke out a whimper of relief. My joy, however, is short-lived because when Tristan moves aside, I finally view the extent of the damage, and I drop to my knees.

I have never prayed, not once during the years I was in the tower. Not for myself or for the parents I lost. I never begged God for my freedom. I simply...existed...never asking for anything, but I clasp my hands, and with my gaze fixed on Quinn, I silently beg God to forgive him for bartering away his soul. To find it in His merciful heart to understand why Quinn made that drastic decision in the heat of a desperate moment. I ask God to please, please, don't let him die because I believe he is a good man.

And we need him to save Rygard.

Also, I need him because I... Because when he touches me, a lifetime of loneliness fades under his hands.

And then I close my eyes, realizing I'm speaking to the wrong deity.

I should direct my pleas to the devil.

"Rapunzel."

My eyes fly open at my name. I spring to my feet, and there's Wren, blood-soaked hand extended at me. Without a thought, I run toward him...

...and throw my arms around him.

To my shock, he hugs me back.

"What happened?" I'm barely able to push out the words.

"John's soldiers happened." He sets me away from him. Rage and worry clash across his face. "They used a poisoned blade on Quinn."

Whatever else Wren says gets lost as my focus shoots to Quinn. I step closer, and there it is. Thick, black sludge pollutes the deep lacerations on his face and throat. "Wren, no."

He grabs me by the shoulders, with his gauntleted fingers biting into me. He shakes me—*hard*. Hard enough that I grit my teeth to keep my molars from grinding. "Look at me." I want to, but I can't tear my gaze from Quinn. "I said fucking look at me, Rapunzel."

My face is wet from desperate tears. Each lungful of air is a battle as panic takes hold of me.

"You need to listen to me." Wren shakes me again, and the jolt snaps me out of my stupor. "John has Sybil."

My bones liquefy. They must, because why else would my entire body slip out of Wren's hold and slide to the ground? But he's right there with me, his hands curled around my upper arms, holding me steady as painful tremors seize me.

"How do you know this?" She was always careful. *Always.*

Wren releases me and shoves my wild hair back from my face. "With the strength and awareness Quinn had left, he told me Stephan of Glasburg led the attack on Haversville. Quinn knew him, and right after he murdered the fucker, soldiers used a tainted blade on him." He cups my face, his gaze silently pleading with me. "That's Sybil's poison killing him. Help him, Rapunzel. Please."

I don't need heightened empathy to know asking me this cost Wren every drop of his pride—not that it should. This is me... and him. And years ago, I was so wrong not to save his father. I may not have fed Percy Kincaid the poison, but withholding the cure made me an accomplice to his murder.

"Take it." I grab a chunk of my hair and hold it out to him. "Take it all to save him."

Take every last strand if it will cleanse my conscience.

Wren's broken smile destroys me. "Hopefully we won't need that much."

Together, we hurry through the group surrounding Quinn. I fall beside Dax, and he pats my thigh. His strength helps to give me the fortitude for what's coming because although I know what to expect when I touch Quinn, nothing can prepare me for when I place a hand on his chest. His agony is a tidal wave crashing through my veins. In its wake flows the living darkness that dwells inside him. That energy is a powerful force, pulling me down... Down so far that if it wasn't for Wren's support behind me and Dax beside me, I couldn't resurface.

"We're running out of time." My words are for no one and everyone. "I need yarrow, comfrey, and woad. Also, a mortar, pestle, and scissors. Hurry." I squeeze my eyes closed. White explodes behind my lids. The commotion whirls around me but slowly dissipates until all I hear is Quinn's body working furiously, but uselessly. Fighting to overpower the venom. When I reopen my eyes, Dax, Wren, and I are the only ones left. But even they fade. I lean low and press my lips to Quinn's ear. "I know you hear me, Quinn Redgrave. Tell that demon he can't have you. You're mine, and I won't give up on you."

Nothing. Not a flutter of his eyelids or a twitch of his lips.

Wren's hands land on my shoulders. I need that comfort as I

smooth Quinn's hair away from his bloody brow and focus on the deep gash that nearly took his left eye. It tears across his forehead and up along his scalp. The sight of such ruination on his beautiful face coils a knot in my gut so tight that my entire body spasms. I wipe the blood from his lips. Then I rasp, "I'm with you, in the darkness and pain." I slip my hand in his. "I know you feel me, Quinn."

Then I seal my words with a kiss.

And there it is.

With the tiniest squeeze from his hand, I breathe out on a small cry of hope.

"He's not...dead?"

I straighten my spine and shake my head at Dax's question. "He squeezed my hand. But they must hurry with those herbs. We're on borrowed moments." Skating on the edge of a sword.

"Fuck." Wren comes around and hits the ground hard next to me. Between these two imposing men, I'm...safe. Strong. Capable. Calm. And when he threatens to join Quinn in hell to kick his ass if he dies, even I laugh at the absurdity of the promise.

Dax joins in, and he and Wren yell at Quinn, demanding that their friend fight. That he better not have the audacity to leave them. With each warning, Quinn's fingers coil tighter around mine as if he's using me as a lifeline to this mortal plane. As if I'm the anchor that holds him here. Saving him from the demon who's come to collect him. A demon that, when I close my eyes, I see in the darkness now that Quinn's suffering has connected us.

Finally, Emma delivers the mortar and pestle. Backing away, she wraps her arms around her torso as silent tears cascade down her ashen cheeks. Everyone is family here, and when one hurts, all hurt. It's not just Quinn bleeding out in this courtyard.

We all are.

There's a commotion behind us as the men rush back. Ian

Twisted

reaches me first, winded from his sprint. I release Quinn's hand in time to catch the large burlap sack Ian tosses at me.

"Is this enough, my lady, or will you need more?"

I peer inside the sack. "Plenty, thank you."

Arthur and Tristan come tearing up next and toss two more sacks at me. I get busy while everyone gathers around to watch me work. Ignoring their watchful eyes, I sprinkle a fair amount of woad into the mortar. Then I add a healthy quantity of yarrow. Last, I pepper in a good measure of comfrey. Satisfied there is enough of each healing herb, I steel myself for what's coming. I pick up the scissors. Lick lips that have gone dry with dread and keep my focus on Quinn's severed throat. I select a lock of my hair. Fit the strands between the sharp shears. Draw deep breaths, and...

...cut.

Knowing Quinn is alive on stolen time keeps me from blacking out. Sybil was always the one who prepared the potion while I broke her heart and sobbed from the pain. I lack that luxury now. Instead, I bite back my cry as the twin blades slice off the golden hair as if they're sawing through a limb. Agony slows my hand, making each second prolonged, with each second crawling over me as the strands snap like tendons. The magic dies at the roots, turning what's attached to my scalp brown. The length in my hand thrives, radiating power. And, barely breathing, I place the severed locks in the mortar and quickly use the pestle to grind it to a fine powder. Within seconds, the mixture transforms into a thick, golden liquid.

"It's ready." My voice is a hoarse whisper the cracks the tension in the charged air around us.

Scowling, Wren sees my suffering, but I give him a curt shake of my head as I hold out the mortar. He takes it from me. "What do we do with it?"

"He drinks it." I'm dizzy from the clash of mine and Quinn's pain.

Dax grabs me when I sway on my knees. I lean against him, trembling. He whispers reassuring words in my ear, believing I'm upset about Quinn. And I am, but I also hurt.

I hurt so badly, but thankfully, the physical pain is momentary and is already passing. The emotional toll, however...

I fear that will linger longer.

But I can't cry. Not now. That can come later when I'm alone.

Tristan positions himself by Quinn's head and props him up as much as possible. Wren puts the mortar to Quinn's mouth. He forces the elixir past his parted lips. Some of the precious liquid spills down his chin, but he still swallows most of it.

We don't have to wait long for the magic to work.

Quinn coughs on the elixir, thrashing violently. Tristan leaps backward, landing on his ass. He jumps to his feet and rushes away, likely afraid that Quinn will wake up swinging.

Wren, Dax, and I stay where we are and watch as Quinn's flesh knits together. First, his face mends, the magic making it as if the blade never sliced him. Then his throat starts to heal, with the outer edges coming together until the entire laceration seals. What's left behind is the scar he already had and his black tattoos.

And then we wait, with bated breath, for him to open his eyes.

Quinn jolts awake and gropes his throat. Wren and Dax grab for him, but Quinn fights them off and springs to his feet. Everyone bolts away, obviously afraid of him. Who can blame them? Quinn is a bloody mess. His hair drenched and his clothing soaked. And there is a feral edge to his black eyes that would even strike fear in the demon waiting for Quinn to join him in hell.

I warned you that you wouldn't take him from me, you sonofabitch.

The joy of Quinn's recovery gives me a reprieve from the

lingering pain coursing through me. That elation makes me the only fool brave enough to walk toward him, arms out.

Unsteady on his feet, Quinn jabs a finger at me. "You." He's still finding his voice and trying to recover some of the breathing denied him from his ruined throat. "I saw you. In the darkness."

"Yes." My nod is jerky, my body trembling as I step closer.

"How was that possible?"

I stop and run my hand over my hair. "I couldn't let you die."

He narrows those black eyes on me and puts a hand to his perfect throat. "I'm damned, Rapunzel. You should have let me die."

"Then should I die as well?" I walk up to him and press my hand to his chest. His heartbeat is strong beneath my palm. "Because we're both cursed, Quinn."

He laces our fingers together, his gaze never leaving mine. "No, Rapunzel. Not you."

Then he pulls me in until our chests slam together and he kisses me. Kisses my forehead, his lips achingly tender. They draw fresh tears to my eyes. He wraps his arms around me, and…holds me. As if he's still using me to anchor himself to life. Because he glimpsed what awaits him, and his panic became mine. His fear a noose around both our necks. He doesn't deserve that, not for giving up something as precious as his soul to save something even more cherished—his sister.

It's not fair.

Like a gate that's thrown open, emotions come rushing in on me. It's all too much. Too much of Quinn's agony while I laid hands on him. Too much of my own when I cut my hair to heal him. Too much horror when I delved into hell to bring him home to us. And it's too many eyes on me when I need privacy to purge this torment from my soul.

I break away from Quinn and run toward the keep. Wren and Dax call my name. Emma does as well, but I keep running. Through the hall. Up the stairs, nearly tripping over the hem of my tunic. I don't stop until I reach my room, and when I slam the door behind me—when I shut out the outside world—it's then that I bury my face in my hands and quietly break apart.

I crawl on hands and knees to a darkened corner. There, hidden in shadows, I curl into a tight ball and twirl a finger around the newly shorn brown tuft of hair, wondering how much of my life I gave to save Quinn's.

Chapter Twenty-Three

WREN

I follow Rapunzel to our chamber. The muted sunlight filtering in through the arrow slit window casts her in shadows. I find her, in the corner, her legs drawn to her chest and her chin resting on her knees. When she sees me standing in the threshold, she slaps away tears as they rain down her flushed face. She shudders in a breath and squares her shoulders, and I swear on God, I've never seen such a stunning display of feminine fortitude.

"How fares Quinn?"

"Already complaining. Emma wants him to rest. He, of course, refused." I close the door before crossing the room. Everything in here now carries her touch. The bed smells of her. There's a trunk at the foot of it filled with her clothes. The open book on the chair near the window belongs to her. Every part of Dyhurst is…brighter…because she's here. I drop beside her. "But he'll live."

She did that.

Gave him back his life.

"We almost lost him." Her husky whisper barely breaks the quiet. We're smeared with Quinn's blood. Exhausted. Her eyes are green pools that reflect my fear over nearly losing my friend. "He was so close, Wren. He was slipping through my fingers."

I want to touch her. To take her hand. Wrap my arms around her. But I don't. Because I'm…afraid. After the terrible names I called her and the accusations I flung at her… I'm scared she'll reject me. "He's alive because of you."

Her smirk could rival my own. "Wasn't Quinn injured because of me?"

And there it is.

Fuck.

"No, Rapunzel, he wasn't."

"Liar." She's shaking so violently I fear her bones will splinter. She digs her fingers in her wild waves and pulls hard enough that even I cringe. "All this destruction. All the death. Because of this cursed hair."

I shift in front of her and pry her hands away and dare to hold them. "I was wrong, Rapunzel. You sacrificed your life for Rygard. This…what John is doing…this is *his* madness. *His* obsession with power. My parents. None of it is your fault."

Shame sits bitter on my tongue at how I hurt her. Of course, she's not to blame. But I needed someone to lash out at, and she was there while John was not. She's someone tangible who could hurt along with me. Someone I could push away. Someone I trusted to be there when I worked through my pain.

Oh, God, did I push too hard? Did I push too far? Did I lose her?

I would rather have Quinn rip out my heart like he did with Stephan of Glasburg than live a life without my Rapunzel.

"But you said—"

"I said many things that aren't true," I interrupt her, my gaze fixed on the stone floor because I can't bear to look at her lest she see the depth of my guilt. "Many things I regret. Too many fucking things I can never *un*say."

Rapunzel leans forward and rests her head on my shoulder.

Twisted

My eyes slide closed, and I swear, each beat of my heart punches harder than the last until I fear it will crack clean out of my chest. "I'm sorry, too, Wren."

"You did nothing wrong."

"But I did." Her tremors ripple through me like a melancholy wave. "You were right about me being a coward. But I couldn't silence Sybil's warnings." She straightens and taps the heel of her palm against her forehead. "They screamed in my head, reminding me to protect my secret. That even the very best of men will use it for evil. I wanted to tell you, but always, the words got stuck because I was afraid." Each word is said on a trembling breath, and when she grasps my hands, she squeezes until our fingers twist. "I should have trusted you. I should have saved your father, no matter the cost."

"You couldn't have saved him, Rapunzel. John would have eventually found a way to murder him. Not even you can alter destiny." This truth kills me to say out loud. Percy Kincaid was too close to John. He knew the king's secret, and John would have hunted him to the ends of the world to protect it. It's a secret I have to tell Rapunzel. But not tonight, when there's too much that still needs to be said between us. And when I pull her on my lap and cradle her to my chest, she sags against me. It's as if she's waited a lifetime for this moment. And maybe she has—because so, too, have I. "I would grant you my forgiveness, but there is no guilt for me to absolve."

Her muffled hiccup damn near breaks me. I wrap my arms around her and hold her, rocking her until the last of her sobs subside. Until she's no longer trembling. Until she finally swats her hair from her face and gazes up at me, her expression raw. It slices my heart in half.

One part beats for me, the other for her.

"I love you, Wren."

I feather a kiss over her lips. "And I've never stopped loving you." I cup her face, my gaze bouncing from the newly shorn brown wisps back to her captivating green eyes. "When it's cut, do you feel it?" Because it looked like she was in agony.

Rapunzel answers with a curt nod.

"Badly?" I press.

"Like severing a limb." Her admission is so quiet, I need to strain to hear her.

Fuck. "And you suffered this pain for Quinn. Why?"

"I couldn't watch him die." Her expression is heartbreaking. "The three of you are too special to me to lose."

"Rapunzel..." Her name slips from my lips like a prayer. She slaps my hands away when I run my fingers through her hair.

"Don't touch it." She scrunches her face in disgust. "It's cursed."

"It's perfect." I ignore her weak protests and bury my hands in the heavy, golden waves. "As beautiful as the rest of you."

She's skeptical. No matter. I'll make Rapunzel love her whole self since I'm a large part of the reason she hates the magic that lives within her.

"I need to tell you something, Wren."

Expecting the worst—ready to forgive her for anything—I tense and detangle my hands from her hair. "What is it?"

She swallows hard. Drops her gaze, and I let her stare at the stone floor if that's what she needs to do to spill her secret. "I once asked Sybil what would happen if I cut it off. All of it. I would be free, right?"

Right.

It sounds easy.

Too easy.

Nothing is ever simple with magic. There is always a cost.

"What did she say?"

I tense, waiting for an answer I know I'll hate.

"I should have died with my mother during my birth. That is the natural order." Oh, God. Oh fuck. Stop talking... But Rapunzel continues. "The magic keeps me alive."

Not even you can alter destiny. I dart my gaze from her eyes to her hair as her words tumble around themselves. Finally, they settle, and... The world crumbles to dust around us. I scrub a hand over my face, still trying to make sense of it.

"The magic is like an hourglass, Wren. When the sand is gone..."

She doesn't need to finish because I understand. Fuck, I understand.

Rapunzel loses another piece of her life whenever she cuts her hair. That's why it turns brown. It's her natural color. The magic...dies...and with it, so does she.

Suddenly, the only thing I see are those shorter locks of brown among the blonde. Each strand represents a lost...day, month, year...of her life. Then I blink and clear my vision, seeing the long, golden waves as a treasure. Not because of the magic they hold but because of the life they support.

I finger a section of cut hair. "Sybil took this time from you."

If I possessed Quinn's power to rip the life from someone, I would tear Sybil's soul to shreds for stealing this from Rapunzel.

"You misunderstand." She's shaking her head, a tender smile lifting her lips. "The magic keeps her healthy and alive so she can protect me."

"Does she have a care that she's fucking killing you?" Not to mention hurting Rapunzel each time she cuts a piece to benefit herself?

"Wren, stop." Rapunzel places her hands on my shoulders. "Sybil did what she must to keep me safe. She didn't want to, but it was our only option."

Jaw clenched, I grind my teeth until my molars damn near crack. "Except one of you wasn't slowly killing the other."

Rapunzel traces her fingers along my brow to smooth away my scowl. "As I said, it was a necessary evil. If she had died, I would have been *truly* alone in that tower."

"You should have come away with me."

Rapunzel surprises the hell out of me with her swift agreement. "You're right. But I didn't. Now we need to focus on getting her away from that madman. You know the depravity he's capable of, just as I know the extent of Sybil's power. She's strong, Wren. Stubborn as well. She can hold John off for a time, but eventually, she'll break—if she hasn't already—and when she does, there's a chance he won't need me anymore."

What goes unspoken is that if Sybil granted Rapunzel the ability to heal...what other power can she give him?

I kiss her again. A peck—because I can. Because she's in my arms, and she's mine. I spent twelve years imagining the day when I could touch my lips to hers whenever I fucking pleased. "We won't give him the chance. I swear it to you. I once promised you that nothing would come close to the adventures you and I would have once you were free. Do you remember?" At her nod, I smile, this time a genuine grin. "You were adamant you would never leave that tower, yet here you are. Why is that, do you think?"

"Because John is destroying Rygard."

"No, Rapunzel." I *tsk*. "Because I'm a determined man whose word is his bond. I vowed to free you from the tower. Now I swear on my life that I'll free you from John."

And when I claim her mouth, I do it with a secret sitting on my tongue—one that will shatter Rapunzel.

But Dax, Quinn, and I will be here to put her back together.

Chapter Twenty-Four

RAPUNZEL

There's something desperate—even feral—in Wren's kiss. It sends me spiraling. I part my lips when he licks his way inside my mouth. It's nothing like Dax, whose kiss was an easy, playful seduction full of teasing and mischief. Or Quinn's rough and primal command of my body. With Wren, the world drops away. The lost years fade. His resentment, a barrier more formidable than the highest, thickest of walls, crumbles to dust. The room becomes a blur, leaving Wren the only tangible thing in my world.

On Wren's lap and cradled in his arms, I don't care that we're still soiled with Quinn's blood. What matters is that today ends a bleak chapter in our story. Every stroke of Wren's tongue across mine writes a new word. Each whisper of his lips over my flesh is a new sentence. Every breath we take is the promise of a new adventure.

My Wren will always be the grubby boy who traveled through rain, sleet, and snow to my tower. He will always be the boy who kept a peony in his pocket for eight years, waiting for the day when our fingers touched in the exchange. He will always be my first love. But now, we're part of something larger than ourselves. Something...*more*. Together with Dax and Quinn, we are complete.

Without breaking our kiss, Wren brings us to our feet. There's laughter when we get tangled in my skirts as he walks us backward toward the four-poster bed. His hands stay busy, roaming down my sides. They scrape over the outer curve of my breasts. Skid over to my ass, where he squeezes and kneads. And when we reach our destination, he gathers the linen skirts of my tunic and chemise to draw the material up my legs...

...then drops them to lean away. Wren tucks an errant tuft of hair behind my ear. "I waited a lifetime for this." He runs a fingertip reverently over the bridge of my nose, then to my lips. "To kiss you."

"Why stop?" God, I hope the answer won't bring this moment to a tragic end.

"I wanted to be your first kiss." A flash of regret dances across his chiseled face. "If I wasn't such a stubborn fucking—"

"Wren." I cover his mouth with my hand, the press of his soft lips a tickle against my palm. "You may not have been my first kiss, but you will be my first in *another* way."

He lowers my hand, the arrogant kick of a brow sending a delicious flutter in the pit of my stomach. "What *other* way, Rapunzel?"

I flick my gaze at our bed. "Quinn and Dax... They saved a part of me for you." When I look back at him, Wren gifts me with my favorite thing in the world.

His smile.

It shines on me like the sun. Leaving these men would be the worst form of torture. Worse than condemning me back to the tower. Worse than forcing me to spend an eternity in darkness. Wren, Quinn, Dax... They infuse me with life far stronger than the magic within my hair.

"Did they?" There's a playful note in Wren's question. "How thoughtful."

"Wasn't it?" I give him a sheepish grin.

Then his eyes turn devious, and his expression takes on a primal edge. "I will always be able to claim you were mine first, Rapunzel."

There it is.

Wren may not mind sharing me with Quinn and Dax, but he also enjoys having something with me that belongs to us and us alone.

I smooth my thumbs over his brow. "You've always had me, Wren. From the day you stepped into the glade, and I peeked down at you from the window. Not a moment has passed since when I haven't been yours."

He grabs my upper arms and squeezes at my confession. I bite my lower lip, sucking in a sharp inhale. "I'm never letting you go again."

"There will never be a need."

Gently, he presses me backward to sit me on the edge of the bed. He stares at me for a moment—just a beat—as if I'm a fragile work of art. "Rapunzel..." Wren, eyes on mine, fingers the laces of his breeches.

"This is what you do to me." He palms himself through his pants. "I want you so fucking bad."

I slide back on the mattress. Part my legs and hitch up my skirts to expose my legs. All the while, I keep my gaze fixed on him. "Then take me."

Challenge accepted, Wren's expression practically screams as he kicks off his boots. I move to shuck my clothing, but he stabs a finger at me. "Don't you dare." Then he shakes his head. "I've been waiting too long to do that myself. Don't deny me my right."

My stomach flip-flops. "I wouldn't dare deny you anything in this chamber."

His smirk tells me he doesn't miss the limitation I put on my obedience. "Damn right, you won't. You're my gift to unwrap."

Despite his trembling fingers, Wren quickly finishes unlacing his breeches. His pants part, and I watch—fascinated and eager—as he draws them past his hips. His cock springs free. My God, it's beautiful. Long. Thick. And so hard. The vein that runs the length of his shaft pulsates. I can't imagine he will fit himself inside me while craving the pain as he tries.

After he removes his shirt and casts it aside, I look my fill of his spectacular body. Strong and muscular, there is no trace left of the lean hunter I remember. In his place is a man built for battle. And when he moves closer, I study the nicks and scars that decorate his sun-kissed flesh. One day, he'll tell me of his life since leaving Leeds. But not today. Today—now—he keeps to his vow of unwrapping me.

Almost in awe, he peels away first my ruined blue tunic. Then my cream chemise. He falls to one knee and teases his fingers along the waistband of my underwear. "Lift up, Rapunzel."

His voice is a gruff command. I obey, and when I do, he slides the garment past my hips and ass. Down my legs. And with a wicked grin, he tosses them away. With him gloriously naked, he gently pushes on my shoulders until I'm supine on our bed. He is tightly coiled power above me as he claims the spaces between my thighs. His body chases away the castle's damp chill, as together, we could set the world on fire.

Everything about him is a stark contrast to me. Where I'm small, soft…delicate, Wren is solid. Carved in stone. I dance my fingers along the unyielding planes of his chest. Across scarred flesh stretched taut over muscle. I ache to reach into his past and erase the memories that must haunt him of when he received those wounds. But that's beyond my magic. All I can do is replace them with better memories as we build our future—just as he always wanted.

Then Wren's mouth is on mine and thought abandons me.

His kiss is greedy. Demanding. Mindful of crushing me, he

props himself on one arm. He teases my breast with his other hand, fingers playing over my fevered flesh. I arch into his touch when he rolls my nipple, pinching it into a tight bud.

"Stay still." He commands, removing his hand like a punishment for my body's reaction.

I reach for him. He shakes his head with a smirk. With a single finger, the tormentor he is, he traces his way from my bottom lip over the curve of my chin. Down my throat. Then returns to my breasts. He circles first one pebbled nipple, then the other. Flicks it with his tongue. Blows on the wet to pull a slow sigh from me.

"Oh, God, Wren... What are you doing?"

His hooded eyes are full of desire. "Anything I want."

To prove his boast, he devours my breast. What begins as a needle prick of desire blossoms into a delicious ache when his hand settles between my thighs. The heat of his palm scorches me as I buck my hips to chase his fire.

Too soon, his mouth is gone and he's watching me with a sly grin. "I remember the first time I pleasured myself thinking about you. Do you want to know when?"

"Yes." My voice is dry as old parchment.

Wren's torturous finger is now sliding along my slit. "We were thirteen. It was one of the days you sat with your leg dangling from the window. Fuck, Rapunzel. It drove me crazy when you sat like that. I was afraid you'd tumble, and I wouldn't be able to save you. Little did I know..." With a tsk, he gives my pussy a playful slap. Then he strokes my clit and pulls a soft sigh from me. "But *that* day, I couldn't stop staring at your perfect leg. And after everyone fell asleep..." He takes his hand from between my legs. Mirrors his words with actions, stroking his erect shaft. "I fucked my hand with the vision of you in my mind."

Oh, God...

"How often did you think about me, Rapunzel?" He pumps slowly, his thumb smearing the pearl of cum leaking from the tip.

"All the time." The admission falls easily from my lips. "Thoughts of you were all that helped me endure those years."

He keeps stroking himself, the sight mesmerizing. "I'm sorry I allowed my grief and anger to come between us."

"That was before, Wren. This is now." Desperate for him, I replace his hand with my own. He's warm velvet over steel. "There's nothing between us now."

Wren locks his jaw, a hiss issuing between his clenched teeth as I glide my hand over him. He rocks his hips in time with each pull on his long length. I squeeze the engorged head, using his precum to smooth the slide from base to tip. Again and again. Until beads of sweat break out on his brow. Until his breath comes in labored huffs that whisper across the stone walls of our chamber.

"Fuck, Rapunzel."

He grabs my wrist, but I wrench it away. I wrap my arms around his back, the ridges of the lash scars rough against my palms. His flesh against mine sparks an inferno, blazing a trail through my veins.

"Please…"

"Please what, Rapunzel?"

Ever the arrogant warrior.

"Please." I buck my hips against his hard cock. "Fuck me, Wren."

"Those words are poetry on your tongue." Wren rewards me by taking hold of the base of his shaft. He rubs his swollen head along my soaked lips. "I wanted to taste you first, make this last, but I've waited too long to feel your cunt around my cock."

"No more waiting," I breathe.

I rock into the cruel tease of his erection. He uses his tip to part me, building the painful pressure of anticipation in my womb. My muscles contract as a rush of desire flows to ease his entry. I'm saturated. It drips from me to slick my thighs. Wren feels it, too, and at his arrogant smile, I bury my hands in his hair and give it a yank to bring his face closer. I capture his mouth in a rough kiss, my frenzied passion combining with his.

"Sure you're ready, Zee?" he growls against my lips. "We can stop…"

"Don't you dare." I release his hair to grip his ass and pull him forward.

He sinks into me, one extraordinarily agonizing inch at a time. Stretching me. Filling me. He fits us together. Makes my body sing until the pleasure almost overrides the pain.

"I'm hurting you."

I swallow hard and blink away the sting of tears. "Only a little."

It's a tiny lie.

He stills. "Then why are you crying?"

"Because I've wanted this for so long." It's all I thought about during those long and miserable nights alone in the dark in that tower. Never daring to imagine that one day, the fantasy of this moment would become a reality. "Wren, please don't stop."

I hitch in a breath, exhaling on a sob as he rocks his hips against mine. His serious expression is etched from stone. His brow furrows as he drives in farther, and with one last brutal thrust, he tears his way fully inside me.

Oh, God. "I never thought anything could feel this good."

"You were made for me." He kisses me urgently. As if I'm his next breath.

He withdraws until he nearly pulls out of me…only to slam back in until I swear, I come undone. Wren does this again and again. His rhythm awakens something primitive in me. Something that demands…more. It demands everything from him— every thrust. Every filthy promise he's rasping in my ear. Every panting breath. All of him. All of us.

"That's it, Zee." The next punch of Wren's hips sends a jolt through me. "You're so close." Another hard lunge seizes the muscles in my body. "Come for me, Rapunzel." He rocks into me ruthlessly. "Look at you. You're exquisite." One more shove sends a tidal wave crashing through me, washing me over a cliff. I hold fast to Wren and ride this warm, wonderful wave as ripples of pleasure shoot across every nerve.

But the tide recedes, and the world slams back into place. Wren's tempo builds, his thrusts long, deep, and punishing. I lift to meet his movements. Work him to find the same pleasure he gave me. He drops his forehead to mine and growls my name. In answer, his slides off my tongue in a ragged whisper. Then, with one last push of his hips, he finds his release inside me.

"I take it this means you're friends again?"

Wren and I both whip our heads toward the door. Dax fills the threshold. Of course.

"The very best of friends, you fucking voyeur." Wren isn't at all surprised by Dax's presence. Then his kiss-swollen lips kick up in a wicked grin. "Enjoy the show?"

Dax cups the bulge of his crotch. "Immensely." He strolls inside…with Quinn pushing his way in past him.

"You had your fun with Rapunzel." Quinn, freshly bathed with his hair still wet, reminds me of a man on the verge of battle. "Move aside, you greedy prick."

"Grumpy fuck," Wren whips back, but he rolls off me, leaving me chilled. And vulnerable. I move to reach for the blanket to cover myself, but Quinn's glare stops me cold.

With them, I'm safe, and although Quinn told me I'll find no love here, he was wrong. The way they look at me leaves no doubt they care for me. And for now, that's enough.

For now.

Wren's eyes roam over Quinn, lingering on his fully healed throat. "You're…good?"

Quinn fingers his perfect throat. "It's as if the injury never happened." His black gaze bounces to me. "Thank you."

What goes unsaid—what does not need to be spoken—is that he's thankful for more than me saving his life. Quinn is grateful I gained him a reprieve from hell.

I climb to my knees, my hair hanging around me. The yellow ribbon Dax tied around it is long lost by now. For once, I don't regard the golden waves as a curse. "You're welcome." Then I add with a cheeky smirk, "Please avoid tainted blades in the future. That was most unpleasant."

Quinn puts a hand to his heart and bows at the waist. "Pardon the ever-loving-fuck out of me, Rapunzel, for nearly dying." The arrogant man straightens and lifts a brow and stalks closer to the bed. "Allow me to atone for my grievous sin, Princess."

An impish Quinn? How delightful. I play along and run my tongue across my lips, my gaze fixed on his crotch. "You can try."

"Saucy wench." Dax comes to stand beside Quinn, and my God, what a pair they make.

The mattress shifts as Wren climbs off to tug on his breeches. It's a dichotomy of actions as Quinn reaches behind his head to gather his shirt. He pulls the white material over his head and tosses it aside. I'm transfixed as he shucks his clothes, his naked body a wonder of strength and power. I've sampled a tiny portion of what rages inside him, and I came away with a newfound appreciation for the constant battle he wages to keep the darkness contained.

"Come here to me," I beckon, and when he kneels on the bed in front of me, his decorated flesh is hot beneath my palms. "Never scare me like that again."

Quinn brings his face close enough for our lips to brush. "Never again."

"Swear it on your heart."

He places a hand on his chest, then on mine. "I fucking swear."

Quinn's lips devour mine, his hands steadying me as a naked

Dax dips the bed when he climbs behind me. Caged between their muscled bodies, I turn when a guttural groan draws our attention to Wren. He's watching from across the room, reclining on the chair. Shirt off, laces of his breeches open. He's cast in shadows, yet his gaze is a physical touch.

Quinn's solid chest is flush with mine. His lips graze my ear. "Do you want to get fucked by us, Rapunzel?"

"God, yes." A rush of pressure builds between my legs, sending a flood of desire dripping down my thighs.

"Good girls get fucked hard. They get filled with cum. And *very* good girls..." He licks the upper shell of my ear. "Beg for their men to fuck them in every hole." His teeth pull a cry from me and my knees go weak for a moment at the shock of pleasure and pain.

Then he's kissing my throat over his bite. His hands are... everywhere. Dax, his stiff shaft pressing against the small of my back, lifts my hair to kiss the nape of my neck. He feathers his lips along the line of my shoulders. His deft fingers tease down my spine. Then lower...

Much lower. Burning a path to my ass. He trails along the crack, pulling a small gasp from me when he circles *that* hole. "Dax?" Panic laces his name as it falls from my lips.

"Trust me, Little Captive." His purr sends a trail of chills over my flesh. "You'll love this."

To my shameful delight, I believe him.

He glides a finger along my slit. To my frustration, he doesn't enter me, merely soaking his finger, then returns to my ass. Tormenting that hole in slow, maddening swirls. I tense and hitch in a nervous breath, but Quinn cups my chin. Then his hand moves lower to clamp around my throat, forcing me to hold his gaze.

"Look at me, Princess." Those abysmal black eyes trap me in a spell more powerful than any witch could weave as Dax works the tip of his finger inside me. It's shocking but not...unpleasant. "That's it. Relax, Rapunzel."

"Fuck," Dax rasps behind me. "Quinn, goddamn. Wait until you're inside her here."

Quinn's mouth lifts in a devious grin. "Soon enough, I will be. Once she's broken in and ready for me." He leans in and brushes his cheek against mine. "Isn't that right, Rapunzel?"

"Yes," I breathe.

Quinn shocks me by plunging two fingers inside my cunt. I scramble to grab his arm, his hand squeezing harder around my throat as the force of dual manipulations jostles me. I cry out with Quinn impaling me from the front and Dax partway spearing my ass. Dax winds a length of my hair around his hand, fisting the heavy mass. He pulls it, jerking my head back as Quinn withdraws his soaked fingers. He brings them to my mouth.

"Open."

I follow his command, and he makes me lick them clean when I do.

"Tell me what you and Wren taste like."

We are... "Divine."

Quinn's mouth curves into a devious grin at Wren's sharp breath. "Good girl." He releases my throat to stroke his cock—with Dax behind me, pushing in a little deeper with each slow thrust of his finger.

But Dax releases my hair, and when my gaze falls on Wren, I almost weep at how he's rubbing his erection. It's too much, and I push back just a little as Dax works farther in my ass.

"Do you want more, Rapunzel?" Wren's voice wraps around me like a caress.

I nod slowly, euphoric from the foreign sensation. "Yes."

"Of course you do." Dax drives in deeper. "You're so perfect." Then he says to Quinn and Wren, "She's squeezing my finger so hard, she's damn near breaking it."

"Fuck," Quinn growls. "Bend her over. I can't wait."

"You heard the man." There's a hint of amusement in Dax's tone as he withdraws his finger. The loss leaves me empty again. "Bend over for us, Little Captive."

Right now, if they asked me to grow wings and fly, I'd give it my best if it meant this pleasure would never end.

Quinn moves back to give me space. Dax puts a hand between my shoulders to guide me forward. I lock my elbows and land on my palms, my ass facing Dax—my face inches from Quinn's massive erection.

"Wren." Quinn's voice is smoke and shadows in the fading sunlight. "I'm jealous of Dax's view of our girl."

Our girl.

A wonderful sense of belonging wraps around my heart.

"So am I." Wren's admission cuts through the small distance between the chair and bed.

"I must admit, it's a wonderful view," Dax boasts. "Come, Wren. See how her pussy drips from you."

Wren comes up behind me, and I glance over my shoulder at him and Dax. My cheeks heat with wanton need under their hot gazes. "I've never seen anything as beautiful."

"And she's ours." The note of pride in Dax's tone sends a flush of heat through me.

"Eyes on me, Princess," Quinn demands. I whip my attention back to him a moment before the sharp sting of a slap lands on my ass. Gasping, I try to rise, but Quinn grabs me by the nape of my neck. "Did I tell you to move?"

"No," I choke out.

"You stay as you are." Faced down, I can't see what's happening, but I cringe in anticipation when Quinn demands, "Smack her again. Harder. For me."

Oh, God…

The second slap rips a cry from me. But a kiss assuages the

pain. Already, I recognize the differences between each man. Dax's hand struck me. Wren's lips eased the pain.

"I'm going to tear your ass apart." *I hope so.* Quinn's gruff promise has me wiggling my backside for more. More of everything.

Quinn releases me, and I lift my head. His beautiful, massive cock is so close. I open my mouth, and he pushes his way in as if it was as natural as breathing.

I suck him as deep as I'm able—and then more, fighting against my gag reflex to rip gruff sounds of pleasure from him. And when Dax nudges my slick entrance with his cock, I moan as his wide tip stretches its way inside me. The old wooden bedframe protests under the weight of our bodies as Dax fills me. He's massive, and I'm still sore from Wren. It takes my body a few moments to accommodate his size. Once it does, he grips my hips and finds his tempo. Pushes me forward, moving my mouth along Quinn's shaft. It's a shove and pull momentum, and although I'm caught between these powerful men, they've given me control.

I can stop this at any time.

Never.

Quinn twines my hair in his hands to hold it out of my way. He's rasping out barely coherent words as I work him into a frenzy.

"You are stunning with Quinn in your mouth and Dax in your cunt." Wren's lips brush the shell of my ear, his breath a whisper over my flesh. "The day will come when we'll fill you together. You want that, don't you?"

I moan in answer and wiggle my ass against Dax's cock. This pulls a hiss from him as he slams into me.

"Her nipples, Wren," Quinn grits out. "Hurt them."

I cringe and whimper when Wren punishes my breasts in Quinn's stead. He twists and pinches the already aching peaks. But he doesn't stay there long. His hand moves to my pussy, with his strong fingers playing in the wet around my clit. Drawing slow circles as Dax drives into me.

"She's so close, Wren." Dax doesn't break his rhythm. "Get her there."

"That's it, Zee." Wren's voice is hoarse, coaxing me to my climax. "Come for us again. Show us how good we make you feel."

His words are the sprinkle of magic that has nothing to do with my hair and everything to do with the heart.

I roll my hips. Push back to chase Dax's cock each time he draws himself almost entirely out. Moaning around Quinn when Dax fills me with his thick, long shaft. Then Quinn's hands tighten in my hair to hold my head steady. He growls my name and fucks my mouth to find his release. I swallow the ropes of cum he shoots down my throat. When the last of it is spent, he stretches his muscled arm toward a bedpost, panting as he grabs it to steady himself. And as Dax spills into me, the familiar tide comes rushing back. My orgasm takes me on another warm and wonderful ride—leaving me to coast in the aftermath wrapped in Wren's arms.

Before Quinn and Dax leave us, long after we've all come down from the glow, they kiss me hard and possessive—and promise they won't be far. They understand that I spent a lifetime alone, I need to keep the people I love close.

Chapter Twenty Five

WREN

I have regrets.

Many fucking regrets.

Sharing Rapunzel with Quinn and Dax isn't among them.

My relationship with Rapunzel has always been uniquely… ours. It began by chance. We survived because of our devotion to each other—even when pride, folly, and distrust nearly tore us apart. The four of us are stronger together, and as I watch the summer breeze catch in Rapunzel's hair while she toils in the garden with Emma and Arthur, a coil tightens in my gut. Especially when she spies me watching her from where I stand on the lists. She sits back on her heels and waves to me from across the courtyard. Her radiance breaks the gloom of the dreary afternoon.

The weather is fitting for the news I have to deliver.

I wave back, then gesture for her as I step off the training ground. Yesterday, after Quinn made friends with a poisoned sword and then we… Needless to say Rapunzel rose well after sunrise. Once she was awake, I invented at least a dozen excuses to avoid her. But each moment that passes breaks our promise of a precious new beginning. One built on respect and trust.

"She needs to know." Quinn follows me off the lists.

I keep walking, although I'm still in awe of how there isn't a trace of the fatal injuries left on his body. "How much did you hear when you were supposed to be dying?"

"Bits and pieces, but it was enough."

Some men, when faced with death, get desperate. Desperation pours confessions from doomed lips. One of Glasburg's men survived my arrow—but barely. He was, shall we say, chatty, with his dying breath and spewed information John has murdered many men to keep secret. Among those slaughtered was Percy Kincaid.

I pull off my gauntlets and scrub a hand over my face. "This is going to destroy her."

"You're wrong." Quinn sheaths his sword and watches Rapunzel stroll toward us. "Make no mistake, Wren, I was a single heartbeat away from death when that woman pulled me out of hell. Literally." Then he raises a brow. "She's strong, and she has us behind her."

"Behind her?" I drawl. "I remember not long ago when you claimed a woman should know her place."

He glares at me with those coal-colored eyes. "Fuck you. I don't recall."

"How convenient." Then we reach Rapunzel, and fuck, I'm about to decimate her pretty smile. She steps up on her tiptoes and brushes her lips over mine before settling back on her flattened feet. Then gives Quinn an equally tender kiss.

"Are you avoiding me, Wren Kincaid?" She swats stray wisps of hair away from her dirt-smudged forehead.

Yes. "No." Her cheeks flame with a charming blush when I take in the bruises we put on her exquisite body last night. "Next time, we won't be so rough." I nod at her throat.

"Yes, we will," Quinn counters.

Twisted

Rapunzel touches the bite marks. Her grin turns from enchanting to devious. "Now that, Wren, would be a true punishment."

I drop my gaze to the juncture of her thighs before tracking back to her face. "Are you sore?"

The woman rolls her eyes and plants her hands on her hips. Her audacity. "Wren, you asked me this twice last night. Twice I assured you I'm fine." And I'm stalling…until Dax joins us, and a frown furrows Rapunzel's brow. "What's wrong?"

"Come with us, Zee." I take Rapunzel's hand and lead her toward the keep.

"Wren, you're scaring me." She falls in step beside me, her icy fingers squeezing mine. Right then, it's as if Rygard weeps for her because the first fat drops of rain fall. "Should I be worried?"

I heave out a sigh as we enter the hall. "We'll talk in our chamber."

Rapunzel digs in her heels and grinds to a stop, causing me to jerk her arm. Her gaze darts between us. "You'll tell me now."

I glance at Ian, Tristan, and Kenric, who are busy in the hall. Before I answer her, however, Quinn comes to my rescue. "Upstairs, Rapunzel. Now."

"Dear God." She slaps a hand over her mouth, her following words muffled. "Sybil is dead. John killed her. Or…"

Dax shakes his head, cutting her off. "No, Little Captive." Then he drags a hand through his unruly blonde hair. His eyes are twin gray storms. "We have no reason to believe the worst."

Yet.

Rapunzel drops her hands and draws in a sharp, fortifying breath. Then she takes the lead and walks *us* to our chamber. Dax guides her to the bed, and when she sits on the edge of the mattress, she worries her hands. Dax sits beside her, not touching her, but stays near enough that if she needs him, he's ready.

Quinn stands beside the bed, leaning against one of the thick wooden posts, arms crossed over his broad chest. He's coiled so tight; his tension is a living entity around us. His black eyes stay locked on her. I stand before her, fingering the hilt of my sword, the weapon a comfort because never in my life has my heart hammered this hard and this loud.

"Wren, please—"

"The constable who burned Haversville is the same prick who oversaw almost every attack in Rygard." My gaze flicks to Quinn because it was his childhood friend—his sister's former betrothed. "Stephan of Glasburg was John's right hand. He was also the bastard who slipped the poison into my father's wine."

Her wide, green eyes fill with tears. "Wren…" My name is a pained wail. "Oh, God, Wren, I'm sorry." Then her expression shifts from anguish to puzzlement. "But why would he offer you this information, knowing you would kill him for what he's done?"

"He didn't. I did." A muscle tics in Quinn's jaw at his boast.

"I didn't get the chance," I say—both of us simultaneously. "And it would surprise you what sins a man will absolve himself of when on the precipice of death."

"Most men also shit themselves." Dax isn't lying. I've witnessed my fair share of men empty their bladder and bowels on the battlefield.

"Quinn killed Glasburg before I got there." If Quinn wants her to know the gruesome details, he can tell her another day. "I felled two men in Haversville. One died instantly. The other… lingered…long enough to confess certain secrets regarding John."

Her brows furrow in confusion and anger. "Secrets worse than murdering your father?"

"Yes, Rapunzel."

She's gripping her hands together hard enough to turn her knuckles white. "I see." Then, in the pregnant silence, she reads me with those perceptive green eyes because, after all these years, she's one of three people who know me best. "This secret is about me."

"Yes." I don't want to drag this out because after twenty-four years of being fed a lie, Rapunzel deserves to know the truth. But I find this moment more brutal than any battle I've fought. I go to her and pry her fingers apart. Hold them in mine. "John sent his most trusted soldiers out with a warning. The king's exact words to them were, 'If even one precious hair on my daughter's head is harmed, I'll cut your throats myself.'"

Rapunzel stares blankly back at me for a moment, the implication not yet hitting her. Until it does, and it's heartrending to see the array of emotions play out across her face. Confusion. Comprehension. Denial. Finally, anguish. Her mouth falls open, then closes. She stands, forcing me to drop her hands. Dax and I rise with her. Quinn backs away a step to give her space. But she changes her mind and sits. She shakes her head and presses a hand to her chest as if to calm her racing heart. Or to soothe a terrible pain. Her frantic gaze bounces to Dax, then Quinn, silently pleading with them.

"John is delusional." The tremble in her voice betrays her brave facade. "That man is not my father. I refuse to accept this."

Dax strokes her face, his somber compassion pulling a heartbreaking whimper from her. "Yes, Rapunzel, he is."

Unshed tears pool in her eyes. She covers Dax's hand with hers and shakes her head. "My father is dead." Rapunzel spins. Her beseeching expression slices me before moving to Quinn. "Why would Sybil lie to me?"

Quinn sits beside her and pulls her into his arms. I don't know how she survived all those years in the tower. It was too much to expect from anyone, much less a child. And now this… to force this on her…

It's not fucking fair.

"For so many reasons." I never thought I would defend the

witch, but here I am, doing exactly that. "But when we get her away from that fucking madman you can ask her yourself."

It takes Rapunzel a few moments to find her fortitude. When she does, she squares her shoulders, her spine a steel rod. There's still a world of pain buried in her eyes, but when she faces me, I see the strength and courage she'll need to meet the challenges ahead of us.

But for a moment—just a flash in my mind—she's the little girl who rose up in the window like the dawn. Her hair a curtain of gold behind her. I loved her the moment I laid my eyes on her. I love her now. And I'll love her the whole of my life.

"If it's true that John is my father..." She touches her head, where a crown would sit. "I'm Rygard's rightful heir."

Quinn scrubs a hand along the sharp line of his jaw. "He would need to confirm this—claim you—in front of witnesses."

She chews the inside of her cheek a moment, then nods. "Fine. Let's find the proper witnesses and get the deed done." She tilts her head and glides her determined gaze from Quinn, to Dax, to me. "That monster will not sit on the throne after everything he took from us."

My parents. Rapunzel's freedom. Quinn's sister.

And still... "No," I hear myself counter before my mind catches up to my mouth.

Dax raises his brow. "No?"

"At no point will Rapunzel be in the same room with that fucking madman."

"Wren, you didn't pull me from the tower only to bring me this far." Rapunzel rests her hands on my chest, my heart hammering against her palms. "There will be risks no matter the plan." She places a finger over my lips when I try to protest. "I can't be killed, remember? And I'm the one who can get close to him. Don't rob me of the right to fight for my own life."

Each word bleeds me because she's right. Goddamnit. John made Rapunzel a part of his fucking game of greed the day his thirst for power overruled his heart. First, he blamed her for the death of his wife. Now he's obsessed with using her to make himself damn near immortal. If Sybil hadn't faked the infant's death and taken her to the tower... I can't even think about what Rapunzel's life—what all of our lives—would be like if she were her father's captive.

And she's asking me to allow her to throw herself into that fire.

And worse, I have to let her.

"Fine." My growl resonates against the stone walls. "But if even one hair on your precious head is harmed, I'll be extremely displeased."

"When John is dead and the crown is mine, I hope my greatest concern is choosing which of you I'll name as my king." Her comment is lighthearted, meant to ease the tension, no doubt.

"None of us." I kiss the top of her head. "No one will rank higher than you in your kingdom, Rapunzel."

Rapunzel's shoulders sag. "I don't want to be queen at all."

"And that's why you'll be a good one." Dax comes behind her and wraps his arms around her waist. "You won't bear the burden alone, Little Captive. Just promise me you won't name me as your court jester."

Her laughter, sad though it is, is my favorite sound. "That, Dax, would be a waste of your true talent."

He nips at her ear, pulling a squeal from her. "Told you she was a lady, Wren."

"Fuck you, Dax." Quinn slides up to her and grabs her chin. He puts his lips close to hers. "I always knew she was a princess." He kisses her—hard. "Jesting aside, I don't like the idea of you getting anywhere near John. But fuck it all if it's the only way to kill the prick." Then he strokes her cheek. "Mark my words, Rapunzel. I'll burn your kingdom to ash if anything happens to you. Do we have an understanding?"

"We have an understanding."

He gives her a curt nod. "You're ours, and we'll fight to our last breath to protect you."

What goes unsaid is that we're on borrowed time. After we kill John, she'll belong to Rygard. But for now, she belongs solely to us in the calm and quiet days before the storm.

Before the world intrudes.

Before the battle starts and the blood flows.

I think back to that day, all those years ago, when my friends dared me to venture into Blithe Forest. I believed it was cursed. They said an evil witch lived here, hidden among the ancient trees. Folks didn't dare venture too far south from Leeds Village. They never crossed the Merrie River. Not me, though. I was fearless. Reckless. I couldn't be afraid on such a fine day.

The day I met my Rapunzel.

The Journey Will Continue…

Acknowledgments

Frankie: This was the hardest one so far. Thank you for listening to me ramble on about Rapunzel and her renegades as if they were real people. Thank you for taking care our girls while I kept my face buried in the computer to bring this story to life. I love you so damn much, you don't even know.

Jesse and Tyler: Every mom should be so lucky to have such amazing children cheering them on the way you do. I love you so much. It's my privilege to be your mom. I'm so proud of both of you in a million different ways each day.

Cassandra: I got punchy at the end. Thank you for sticking by me and for kicking my ass right up to the 11th hour. I love you like my left kidney. I'm so grateful for your friendship, you have no idea.

Lisa: Here we are again. Only this time, in an entirely different world! Thank you for being with me from the beginning, when I first asked if you wanted to b with me on this roller coaster.

Kerri: The day must come when you and I share the same space because I refuse to accept a world where I don't give you a huge hug and tell you, face to face, how much you've become the sister of my heart.

Lina: It's not because you're Canadian. You're just a genuinely nice person, and I'm blessed that you're my friend. Thank you. You have no idea how many times you've brightened my day without realizing it.

Becca and the the Acourtofspicybooks Club: Thank you for giving me one hell of a fun week—and for allowing me to come away from that wonderful whirlwind with awesome new friends!

Charly: I'm keeping you. Sorry, but it has to be done. Thank you for being the sweetest and kindest of souls.

Samatha Watkins: Thank you for letting me borrow Cassandra. Do we need to work out a joint custody agreement?

Patrons: Oh, my gawd, guys, I adore you! Sorry I got quiet as I raced toward the end of TWISTED, but building this world and tying up plot holes kicked my ass. It's back to normal now, promise.

Sirens: We did it! Thank you for being my friends. My cheerleaders. My support. My voice when I crawl in the writer's cave. You ladies are…everything.

My (awesome) Readers: Wow, wow, wow! Thank you for coming with me on Rapunzel's journey. Many of you have been with me since word one of WRAITH, and now here we are…on this epic ride with Zee, Wren, Quinn, and Dax. My gratitude for you coming along with me is absolutely everything. Every word I write is for you. Every moment spent at my desk, hitting this keyboard, is for you, and you alone. I've wanted to write you stories since I was a little girl. Thank you for letting me share my crazy imagination with you. Without you, I'd be writing into a void.

About the Author

Renee Rocco loves to lose herself in dark romances. She writes complex, damaged antiheroes, pairing them with beautifully tormented heroines. Although she jumps Romance genres, switching between Contemporary with a splash of Dystopian to Dark Fantasy, she got her start in Paranormal. She shamelessly abuses the em dash and ellipsis, and is addicted to bubble tea. By day, Renee works for a NY publisher, with her nights spent indulging in her imagination. Beneath the glamour of work-from-home mom duties, she's a suburban misfit who always has a sarcastic comment at the ready—whether the situation calls for one or not. She's not Instagram-ready or speakerphone-friendly (you've been warned).

Sign up for Renee's newsletter and be the first to receive news and previews. Or join her on Patreon where she's sharing her out-of-print series, the Templar vampires, plus so much more!
https://reneerocco.com

Templar Vampire Series

Only on Patreon
www.patreon.com/reneerocco

Where the damned come to play

With a kingdom at stake,

it's all or nothing for Rapunzel and her renegades.

Rapunzel never wanted this war with her father. Unfortunately, she's learned that people rarely choose their battles—only how bloody they're willing to get for victory.

Return to Rygard!

https://reneerocco.com/twined

Preview of WRAITH

**It's a new world order...
where the villains are the heroes.**

***Mayhem made him a delinquent.
Gomorrah made him a monster.***

Turn the page for a sample of *WRAITH*,
book one in the Masters of Mayhem series.

Preview of WRAITH

START READING!
https://reneerocco.com/wraith

Prologue
Eric

Post–Civil War II
Mayhem, Pennsylvania

"Hi."

I resist the urge to grin when I look up from the textbook resting on my lap. Shielding my eyes against the afternoon sun, I see Jamie Ellis hovering over me. My pulse quickens, and my palms go slick, but she can't know I'm excited. I'm friggin' thrilled, but I'm Eric Shaw, and I have a reputation to uphold. "Why'd you miss school yesterday?"

She shrugs and squats beside me. Adjusts the skirt of her ugly blue dress around bruised legs. The clean scents of soap and shampoo cling to her. "Whatcha reading?"

Most people avoid me. Not Jamie. She's a tiny warrior invading my space. I don't mind, though. We've known each other since kindergarten, but from a distance. Things changed late last semester. I caught Kyle McCarter groping her in the hallway and beat the living shit out of him. When the new school year started, Jamie glued herself to my side. For the last nine months, we've spent every lunch period together.

Prologue

Not going to lie. This girl being in my shadow annoyed the hell out of me at first, but I didn't want to hurt her feelings. I mean, hell, everyone knows she gets beat by her dad. Saw no reason to be a dick to her. Figured she'd go back to keeping to herself. She didn't, and then she grew on me, like mold. My friends accepted her because they knew I'd kick their asses if they didn't.

Now, weekends suck because she can't hang out. Her asshole father locks her up in their house over on Vine Street, only letting her out to go to school and the library.

The thing is, Jamie got dealt a raw deal, and nobody seems to want to do a damn thing about it. But *someone* has to have her back. Standing at over six feet tall and muscular to balance out the height, I'm a big kid. Appointed myself her unofficial bodyguard. At school, anyway. Can't help her when she's at home.

Not yet, anyway.

But I'm working on a plan.

Tiny details about her get me going, and I have to remind myself Jamie's not my girlfriend. Doesn't stop me from wanting her. Can't help it. When you get past the thrift store from hell wardrobe, she's friggin' gorgeous. And other guys see it, too, but they know they have to go through me to get to her and that's not happening.

They're horny, not suicidal.

Can't blame them for trying, though. She's got the cutest sprinkling of freckles on the bridge of her nose. Her green eyes are speckled with what looks like golden glitter. Her face is flawless skin and sharp angles, giving her an almost mythical appearance. Like some fairy-tale creature come to life. Hard to tell if the body buried beneath the ugly, oversized dresses has curves or not, but I'm going to go with no. Personally, I don't give a shit. She's perfect as far as I'm concerned.

What I do notice is that when she's nervous, Jamie wrings her hands until the skin's splotchy, and she scrunches her face

Prologue

into an adorable scowl when she's pissed. And there's the bruises everyone pretends not to see—myself included. She doesn't talk about them, *ever*. Most times, it's like I'm the one person who gives a shit if she's hungry and hurting. I mean, yeah, I can beat the hell out of all the Kyle McCarters in the whole damn world, but I can't do for her what an adult can.

I can't save her from her dad.

But everything changes in two years.

Jamie has to hold on a little longer. Once we're eighteen, I'm getting her away from her father so she can start a life for herself.

I tap the tip of her nose. "A book is what I'm reading, Runt."

Jamie scoots closer until our thighs touch. Her heat seeps through the denim of my jeans, sending a rush of blood to my dick. Because, yeah, what I need right now is a hard-on in the middle of the schoolyard. *Outstanding*. Her hand shakes as she tucks a lock of her shoulder-length hair behind her ear. She tilts her face to the sky, her expression, as always, unreadable. "On sunny days, I can imagine being someplace else. Somewhere clean."

Her head's angle shows a fresh burn the size of a cigarette on her neck, below her ear.

Sonofabitch.

Jamie squeezes her eyes shut, and I give her a quick once-over to see if the bastard did more damage. There's a new, fist-sized mark on her chin. Lip's got a small split, too. My gut tells me if her father keeps this up, he's going to kill her before I have the chance to get her away from him. Then I'll have to kill him, and it'll be a colossal mess.

Maybe it's time my father teaches Billy Ellis what happens to a grown-ass man who uses his daughter as a punching bag.

"I love Mayhem," I remind her for the billionth time.

Jamie opens her eyes and gapes at me for a full thirty

Prologue

seconds before laughing in my face. It's the first time I've heard her laugh—truly laugh—since I've known her.

"Impossible."

"It's true," I counter.

Mayhem is in my blood. My dad's Unholy, and at sixteen, I'm already on my way to following in his footsteps. I'm positive my best friend, Luke Hayden, and I are why Sheriff Warren is a raving drunk with a nervous tic.

"Yes, well, you would. You're Mayhem royalty." She plucks the history textbook off of my legs. "Light reading?"

I shrug. "Finals are next week."

Rusty Shaw is big on school and made me promise I'd graduate. Since I have to be here anyway, I figure I might as well do my dad one better and finish with honors.

If anyone other than Jamie or Luke saw me reading the book, I'd make a joke rather than admit to studying. With her, I don't have to be that guy. My so-called bad-boy reputation doesn't impress her.

She examines the photos of old America splashed across the textbook's glossy page. "Must be nice to be the smartest kid in class."

I work my ass off to get good grades. Hence, studying while I waited for Jamie to walk her cute butt over to me.

"Knowledge is power." I've adopted my dad's motto.

"True." She turns the page and taps the photo of a lit-up and bustling Times Square. "Ever wonder what the world was like before the war?"

"Never."

According to history, the conflict began on social media at the same time a global pandemic killed off a shitload of the world's population. Online mobs created a nanny state that decimated fundamental freedoms. The fighting spilled over into the physical world. Riots erupted. Bloodbaths sparked a Second Civil War. Millions were slaughtered, and America burned.

Prologue

When the battle ended, a fractured nation emerged from the ashes with no real winner and only degrees of loss.

We're still cleaning up the mess, with huge chunks of the country buried under rubble and trapped in chaos.

Jamie sets the book aside and steeples her legs. When she rests her chin on her knees, I get a peek at the black shorts beneath her skirt—and the bruising on her inner thighs.

Christ, no.

My jaw clenches and my muscles stiffen as fury turns my blood to lava. I'm about to ask Jamie the brutal question, already plotting how I'm going to kill Ellis and dispose of his body, when she stops me dead with an announcement that cools my rage and replaces it with dread.

"I'm going away."

No one strays far from Mayhem. The town has its own gravity, grounding everyone who lives here.

I hide my skepticism. Or is it fear? *Whatever.* "Yeah? Where are you going?"

"Someplace I'll hate more than Mayhem."

I want to put my arms around her, but I don't, afraid I'll spook her. Jamie hates being touched. Can't say I blame her. "Stay. Problem solved."

"Can't." She stretches out her legs. There are more marks on her shins. "I came to school to say goodbye and to thank you for being my friend."

Jamie pops onto her knees and faces me. I stay as still as death when she grips my shoulders. I may not be relationship material, but I would be better for her. *Only* for her. Then she surprises the hell out of me by leaning in real close to press her mouth to mine.

I lick the taste of apples off her lips.

As of this second, apples are my favorite fruit.

When Jamie moves away, I'm tempted to haul her back for another kiss. But I don't because teachers are watching, and

Prologue

when she glances over her shoulder, I track her gaze to the squad car parked outside the schoolyard. Her sad smile is a knife in my heart. She stands and brushes dirt off her bare knees. Then she spins on the heel of her scuffed, white Vans, and before I can stop her, she marches toward the school. I should chase after her. Instead, like an asshole, I stay stuck to the spot beneath the tree and watch as she disappears inside the old, brick building.

Time grinds to a halt, but somehow, the minutes still fly by.

Five...

Ten...

The bell rings, marking the end of the lunch period. I grab the textbook and join the student lineup, taking a place behind Luke. He had a growth spurt this year and finally caught up to my height.

"What's the sheriff doing here?" Luke asks over his shoulder.

"No clue," I say, but I have a sick feeling it has everything to do with Jamie.

As we shuffle toward the entrance, Sheriff Warren comes marching out. He's not alone. I don't know what shocks me more —Jamie's kiss lingering on my lips or seeing her led away in handcuffs.

1
Wraith

Eight Years Later
Marion County, Florida

I'm positive of one absolute truth—I'm not dying in this cage.

Bad enough, David Crane makes bank off my fights. I won't give him the satisfaction of profiting from my death.

It's Fight Night, and the Coliseum's ground floor is packed. Rows of chairs ten deep wrap around a steel cage in the center of the prestigious arena. A cloud of tobacco smoke thickens air rank with too much cologne, perfume, and sweat. Strategically placed bouncers serve as crowd control. Provocative, leather-clad bartenders hustle to keep pace with the steady flow of orders. Flirtatious waitresses work an upscale horde, sating the mob's appetite for liquor while fighters quench their thirst for violence.

The action flows to a brothel above the arena. Up there, enough money buys limitless debauchery. Shit those sick fucks do in the luxury rooms is so bad, we won't even allow it in Mayhem—and our motto is *Pick your pleasure*, so…

Yeah. It's fucking disgusting.

Crane built himself a kingdom on the border of Ocala

1

National Forest. As far as I know, there's only one way in or out, making Gomorrah virtually inescapable. But trust I'm getting out of here, and it won't be in a body bag.

Never turn your back on your enemy.

The warning echoes in my head. Keeps me upright long after I should have fallen. My opponent is taller than me, agile, too, but slim. Felix's jabs are quick, but I'm quicker. His kicks brutal, but I'm stronger. The guy has landed more than a few solid hits, and I swear he's ruptured something vital when he roundhouses me. But I'm a brick shithouse and I withstand the battering, giving better than I receive.

Shame I have to kill him. He's putting up a hell of a fight.

Cracked ribs are razor blades grating against my lungs. Sweat stings my eyes. My brain is bashed around inside my skull, with each crash of Felix's fist doing more damage. But I'm still alive.

Mayhem born and raised, I've fought my way to the top of the Unholy's food chain, earning a place as the gang's most feared enforcer. I know how to hurt someone, and I dig deep as I swing my right arm in a heavy overhand, aiming for an imaginary target beyond Felix's head. The goal is never to hit the person. It's to punch *through* them. I aim past him, the slam of my knuckles shattering flesh and bone. Christ, I destroy the man's face, ruining his orbital socket.

I'm relentless. Can't give Felix a shred of mercy. Instead, I bare my teeth, an animal moving in for the kill, and hammer him with a volley of punches until my arms scream from exhaustion.

Concussed, I see three of Felix and maintain the attack on the one in the middle. He crawls away, groping at the mat, and gains his feet. I spit out a mouthful of blood and charge forward. I nail him hard enough to buckle his legs. My guard stays up, and although I never hesitate, I'm still a fucking human being beneath this…monster…and I can't bring myself to whale on a man when he's on his knees.

1

Die, damn you.

There's no glory in my inevitable victory—no honor in beating someone who lost the fight a dozen punches ago. But the battle won't end until one of us is dead.

The crowd's roar is thunderous, their bloodlust sickening. These people are supposed to be civilized members of society. God-fearing, law-abiding aristocracy who glare down their collective nose at folks who live outside of their manicured world. To them, I'm trash—less than nothing. A criminal who, they believe, has earned my place in this cage.

Screw them.

Felix pushes to his feet, his legs unsteady. He doesn't raise his arms. He's not protecting himself, and he's not putting up a fight. A ghost of a grin lifts his bleeding lips. Holy shit, the guy is gone. Checked out. The battering trashed his brain. Completely busted him to hell. It's no consolation to my conscience, but he knew he would die tonight. I saw the defeat in his eyes when he entered the cage. Saw his fear—and ultimately his acceptance—when the door locked behind us. It's a surrender I'd seen on other fighters when they knew they'd lost before the battle began. Doesn't make having to kill this man any easier.

Nor was it easy for me to end the seven opponents who came before him.

Felix's face will make eight I'll never unsee.

Eight men whose blood will slowly drown me until I'm dead.

But not today.

As Crane's current champion, I've become the perfect killing machine. The reigning fan favorite. The main attraction who draws a prestigious crowd. Shit, even Marion County's mayor turned out for tonight's event. Corrupt prick was waiting for me when the handlers brought me up from the dungeon. Claimed he wanted to meet me. *Bullshit.* His actual motive was to warn me that I better win because he has a fortune riding on my match.

Politicians. Gotta love the worthless douchebags.

1

I raise my arm to deliver the killing blow that will put a shit-load of money in Mayor Dickhead's pocket.

The mob chants the name Crane gave me, and it makes my skin crawl.

Atticus. Atticus. Atticus.

The noise disorients me as I tower over Felix. With my fist hovering in midair, I pause. Waiting... Felix gives me a barely perceptible nod. A silent plea to end his agony. The steel links of the octagon close in on me. My heart hammers a punishing beat. I lick chapped lips and taste Felix's defeat mingled with the coppery tang of blood.

I'm fucking sorry, man.
This isn't me.
You sure?

I silence the voice screaming in my head, content with the knowledge that I've never murdered an innocent man until I was brought to Gomorrah and forced into the cage.

Two hundred twenty pounds drives my fist. The punch nails Felix square in the temple. The unstoppable force colliding with a solid object that cracks his skull. Felix's head snaps to the side. His torso twists at the waist. He hangs there, suspended, then tips forward. He hits the mat with a heavy thud.

He twitches.

His body stills.

Blood pools under his head.

Fight's over.

Rage and regret collide when I spin to face Crane. The object of my fury sits front row with his slicked-back blond hair and expensive gray suit. A false idol among mortals. I gnash my teeth and snarl at the crowd, giving them the animal they demand. Politicians and law enforcement pepper the crush of bodies. Greedy bastards are on Crane's payroll, relishing the violence as they applaud my ignoble victory.

1

I may be the weapon, but the crowd crammed inside the Coliseum are equally responsible for Felix's death.

I'm about to turn away, the sight of them repulsive, but a face catches my attention. The world tunnels, and all I see is *her*, sitting beside Crane with an expression as blank as Felix's. She's an understated spectacle in a white dress among the garish mob. A cloud of wavy brown hair tumbles over her shoulders. Angular features remind me of a grown version of someone I forced myself to forget. Someone I can't afford to remember. Not here, because she's my one weakness, and if there's one thing I can't be in Gomorrah, it's vulnerable.

With hands clasped on her lap, the woman watches me, and I swear she can see straight to my fucking soul. Right down to the filth festering inside me. To the monster clawing at my skull, fighting to break free. But there's no judgment in her striking eyes. Those eyes that weave a spell and, bizarrely, calms the rage sizzling through my veins.

Maybe Felix isn't the only man who died in the cage. Maybe she's an angel come to usher me out of this hell.

Nah. I'm in too much pain to be dead.

And I'm sure as shit not bound for heaven.

I earned a place in hell on my eighteenth birthday. The day I became an Unholy.

Spell's broken. I tear my gaze from her and swipe my arm across my eyes to clear away the blood and sweat before flipping Crane the middle finger. Satisfaction is its own reward when the gesture wipes the cocky grin off his tanned face.

Gratification lasts seconds. Exhaustion gets the better of me, and my legs buckle. I land in a heaving heap. My head slams against the mat. I'm less than a foot from Felix's corpse. His eyes are glossed over as they stare at me in frozen serenity.

I flip on my back. The movement takes almost more effort than I have left in me. I blink against the glow of the lights as visions of my life flood my mind. Of nights raising hell with

1

Jester—who was known as Luke before he became Unholy. We're more brothers than friends and spent too many drunken weekends at Sanctum, the Unholy's clubhouse. We stood shoulder to shoulder the day we joined the gang and bled together more times than I can count whenever trouble came knocking on Mayhem's door.

The Unholy may not share DNA, but we're a family, and I know they're tearing the world apart looking for me.

Loyalty. Devotion. That's the only language the Unholy speak. Fuck with one of us, fuck with all of us. Ambush, abduct, and torture one of us… Yeah, you're asking for a special kind of revenge. And when I get out of here, I'm coming back with an army of Unholy to burn this fucking place to the ground.

And I *am* going home.

Question is, which version of me will return to Mayhem—the man I was before Crane took me, or the monster Gomorrah created?

Dread strangles me because of what's coming next. Crane uses liquid pain to keep us compliant. Grudgingly, I admit it's diabolically brilliant.

Medical advances were the one good to come out of America's Second Civil War. Nz822, street name noz, the one everyone calls a miracle drug, lessened a soldier's downtime after an injury. Got them healed and returned to battle within days. They even found it worked on certain types of cancers if the tumor was caught early enough. The government controls it, and that's why there's still cancer. No money in the cure. But Crane knows the right people, and noz flows like water in Gomorrah. He drowns us in it after a fight or torture session. Makes sure we're good and healed so he can hurt us all over again in an endless cycle of pain.

Fun times, man.

Ketaphrin, better known as ket, is liquid agony. It fucks with the brain's receptors, sending out empty pain signals. Labeled a

1

crime against humanity, ket was banned after the war. But Crane has a supply chain for that, too, and uses the shit as an added layer of security. As long as he keeps us pumped with it, we're useless sacks of meat unable to defend ourselves against the sadistic guards.

When the door of the cage flies open, I snap out of my stupor, and my body tenses on instinct. Two handlers storm in brandishing cattle prods. Too battered and exhausted to resist, I lift my arms and offer them my wrists. Compliance doesn't spare me. Instead of binding me with zip ties, Lyle zaps me. I clench my teeth as electricity seizes my muscles and vibrates my bones. The stink of charred flesh sickens me—and gives me two more burns to add to the growing collection.

I struggle not to vomit as the crowd's roar of approval shakes the Coliseum. I remind myself to breathe and work to stay awake. I know what Crane does to unconscious men for the mob's amusement.

It's not pretty.

Lyle kneels beside me, syringe in hand. "Lookie what I got."

I bite back a hiss at the jab of the needle into the side of my neck. Liquid heat slides through my vein, easing the cattle prod's sting. Relief lasts seconds. In its wake comes a flood of knives that rip me apart from the inside out. As always, my dick hardens, pleasure and pain twisting in my mind until I don't know what my body loves more—agony or bliss.

Goddamn ket. When you're on it, the drug makes you need the exquisite torture on a cellular level.

See? Diabolical.

Lyle slaps my head. "You ain't sleeping, are you?"

I fight the urge to kill the prick as I push to my feet. Lyle's not done having his fun with me. A solid kick to the back of my knee nearly puts me back on my ass. I take his measure through the filthy ropes of hair hanging over my eyes. Purely on instinct, I move to lunge at him, but Thomas stops me.

1

His hand clamps on my shoulder. "It's not worth it."
Bullshit.
Even fucked up, I'm stronger than both guards. I can take their weapons easy and beat them half to death before anyone can charge in and stop me. But I don't, because Thomas is right, damn him. The consequences I'll face aren't worth the momentary satisfaction of breaking Lyle's jaw.
Or outright killing the asshole. At least not yet.
"He's a dead man," I growl.
"But not tonight." Thomas, who's only a few years older than me, holds out a zip tie. "Hands, Atticus."
"Not my name." I shove my arms behind me and give him my back.
"It is in here." He binds my wrists and ushers me out of the cage.
Thomas takes the lead, sandwiching me between him and Lyle. Nothing good happens when the little asshole is behind me. My muscles tense at the buzz of the cattle prod a fraction of a second before the contact tips fry me. *Again.* I trip down the three steps of the raised platform as electricity sizzles every cell in my body. My head cracks against a post. Knocked nearly unconscious, I need a second to catch my breath and for my brain to stop vibrating inside my skull.
Laughter resonates around me, but I couldn't care less. I'm beyond humiliation. Nor can I heft myself to my feet. I stay right where I am, my gaze locked on the woman in the white dress. She's too damn pretty for this place, and I can't help thinking I've seen her before. Her face is a faded dream teasing the edges of my confused mind. God, I can stare at her all night. Her flawless face fascinates me. But Lyle tugs at me, and I grit my teeth as I heft myself up.
Crane motions to his bodyguard. The buff henchman takes the lead, and Crane rises from his chair with an air of supremacy. He strolls up the aisle without a backward glance. The woman

1

shoots to her feet and follows him, and she's so small she has to race to catch up with him. A second bodyguard completes their four-person procession as the mob parts to let them pass.

The arena snaps into focus, and I hear Thomas demand, "Seriously?"

Lyle shrugs. "Next time, he'll think twice before eyeballing me."

Thomas rubs his temples in frustration, something he often does around Lyle. The younger guard is a brat who sulks when he's chastised or doesn't get his way. "Hit him again with it, and I'm writing up a formal complaint."

As if that'll do a good goddamn thing.

"I ain't making no promises." Lyle shoves me to get me moving. "Walk, asshole."

I struggle to catch my breath as Lyle pushes me toward the back of the arena. Thomas files in behind me as we cut a slow path through the chaotic horde. My bare feet crunch down on cigar and cigarette butts, spit, spilled drinks, and God knows what else. People don't part for us as they did for Crane. Instead, they close in. Grope me. Pull at my hair. A woman launches herself at me in a blur of too much makeup and not enough clothing. She wraps herself around me, drenching my face with sloppy kisses.

I try to pry her off, but she grips me tighter. Her nails, sharpened to friggin' claws, scratch across my shoulder blades, digging trenches in the skin.

It takes Thomas and Lyle to drag her away.

"No touching," Thomas yells over the noise as he sets her on her feet.

Then we're moving again, with Lyle yanking me along.

"You gotta walk faster," Thomas urges from behind.

The fuck?

Does he think I'm moseying for the fun of it? My legs can barely support my weight.

1

By the time we finally make it through the crush, a guard, dressed head to foot in black tactical gear and wielding an AK-47, opens the steel door at our approach. Beyond the threshold is a corridor leading down to the dungeon. The air in here is thinner, cooler, the noise of the arena muffled. When the door closes, the click of the lock sliding into place is a harsh reality check of the insurmountable obstacles between me and freedom. Impossible hurdles I'd need to navigate to escape this waking nightmare.

Harsh fluorescent bulbs hum overhead as we trek the decline that ends in the building's bowels. Cameras, affixed to the low ceiling, are eyes in the sky watching us as we near the dungeon. The distant slap of leather against flesh mingles with a symphony of cries that grow louder the closer we get to our destination. I can't block out those wails.

Mine, I know, will join the chorus in due time.

I spent my first twenty-four years believing I was invincible.

This place cured me of my delusion real quick.

My arrogance was astounding. I thought Crane couldn't break me. Hell, I even scorned the prisoners who whimpered into the dark long after the dungeon quieted for the night. Naively thought those men were pussies. But Crane and his men are artists when it comes to pain, and our bodies are their canvases.

At the gate, Lyle blows a kiss at the camera. The door slides open, the groan and grind of metal echoing throughout the interwoven corridors.

Once we're past the first barrier, the door bangs closed behind us, sealing us inside the Hub. Two guards man the control booth, protected behind shatterproof glass. One jailer backs away from the window. Does he think I'm stupid enough to try to bust my way in, and what...? Kill them with my hands zip tied behind me? I mean, shit, I'm good, but not *that* good.

"Look who's still with us." Adam's voice sounds from a

1

speaker fastened above the glass. The ballsy bastard gives me a thumbs-up.

"Yep. Atticus done won himself another fight." Lyle claps me on the back over the spot where the woman scratched me. "What's this make, five wins?"

Eight.

"Congratu-fucking-lations. You get extra chow tomorrow," Pete announces.

Outstanding. Two helpings of slop. Can't wait.

"Come on." Thomas grabs me by the upper arm and hauls my half-crippled ass across the large, open area.

"Easy," I hiss.

"Geez, we're just congratulating the man," Adam grouches.

The ket's kicking in hard. The air is hot and stale, and despite the oppressive heat, I shiver as I stumble over my feet. Agony slices at my nerves with a surgeon's precision. I double over, gagging.

Lyle yanks me upright and continues through the dungeon's main chamber. "Ain't got all day."

I straighten and shuffle through the Hub, which branches off into four sections. Three corridors are blocked by steel doors. Lightweights and welterweights are kept together down one unit. Middleweights and heavyweights are housed in another. After I defeated the previous champion, they moved me from there to Elite, and I'm still deciding if the only single-celled unit's solitude is a blessing or a curse.

A gym and a disgusting, sad excuse for a shower is located down the fourth corridor. And at the very end of that hallway is the torture room. It's nasty as fuck in there, with every instrument imaginable to inflict massive damage to a human body.

Can't count how many times I've been inside that room, but it's too damn many.

Thomas unlocks the steel door and pushes it open.

1

Lyle shoves past him and pats his knees while making kissing sounds. "Come on, puppy. Time to get in your cage."

I'm a lot of things, but dumb isn't one of them. However, I'm hovering dangerously close to losing my shit and doing something stupid.

I shuffle over to Lyle. Get up close and personal with the fucker. "One day, you and I are gonna have a go."

By now, I have Lyle figured out. Wasn't hard. The guy is one-dimensional. He's an insecure moron who hides his shortcomings behind false bravado. He wouldn't last a night in Mayhem.

Lyle's Adam's apple bobs when he swallows. "You threatening me, Atticus?"

My cruel grin is an intimidation tactic, and it works. I can smell the fear on him. "Stating a fact."

Thomas fires his cattle prod but doesn't fry me. "Back off."

Like I give a shit about being shocked again. But the ket takes full effect, and I fight against gravity as pain tries to take me down.

"Dammit," Thomas mutters. "Help me get him in the cell."

Lyle snorts. "I ain't his caretaker."

"Whatever," Thomas snaps. "Go away, Lyle."

Lyle throws a mini tantrum as he huffs out of Elite.

"You can't keep doing this." Thomas cuts the zip ties and holds out his hand.

I slap it away. "I can walk." I limp into the cell. "Lyle's a jerkoff."

"A jerkoff who can make your life miserable."

I grunt out a humorless laugh. "You're kidding, right?"

"I didn't mean…" Thomas lets the sentence trail off. "Can you get on the bed yourself, or do you need help?"

"I got it," I slur.

No, I don't, but I'll be damned if I accept a guard's help—

even if it's coming from Thomas, who's not an asshole like the others.

It takes my remaining energy to climb on the disgusting mattress. The thing is stiff, crusty, and bloodstained. It stinks of urine, and when I settle on my back and fling one arm over my eyes, I fist the other at my side, praying for sleep to come quick.

"What do you need before I go?"

Thomas and I have a strange relationship. Not friends, but not enemies. I'm still killing him along with everyone else in Gomorrah, but until then, he's the closest thing I have to an ally.

"A gun."

"Sleep it off, Atticus."

The cell door slams shut, and his footsteps fade. Lucky prick. He's walking toward freedom and fresh air.

I lie awake and stare into the darkness as I ride waves of agony and reminisce about life's simple luxuries. Hot showers. Warm food. A clean body. A soft bed. And as I finally, blissfully, float off into the abyss, I dream about an angel in a white dress.

START READING!
https://reneerocco.com/wraith